Navajo Creation Myth

The Story of the Emergence - the Diné Bahane'
Legend of the Navajo Native American Peoples

By Hasteen M. Klah

Published by Pantianos Classics

ISBN-13: 978-1-78987-155-5

First published in 1942

Contents

Preface .... *iv*

General Introduction .... *viii*

The Story of the Emergence - *Hahdenigai-Hunai* **21**

Navajo Ceremonial Songs **76**

Hozhonji—Blessing Chant **101**

Notes on Approximate Locations where Navajo Ceremonies are Now Given 106

Glossary of Navajo Creation Myth 108

Preface

Though I had planned not to appear except as a recording agent in this publication of my work of seventeen years, I have been told that it is necessary to give some account of the origin and reason for my interest in the work. I used to go camping in the Navajo region and from guides and other campers heard of Navajo Yehbechai and so-called Fire Dance ceremonies, so with two friends went on horseback from Fort Defiance, Arizona, to Cuba, New Mexico, particularly for the purpose of seeing some ceremonies.

In those days it was almost a matter of luck if one ever could find out about the ceremonies and I was surprised to find that most of the traders, though some had lived long among the Indians, liked them and spoke Navajo, knew nothing and cared less about their religion; and among the school teachers this was the usual attitude. We happened on a Yehbechai near Chin Lee, then crossed the Chuskai mountains and came down to Newcomb, a small trading-post facing the desert with its only link to civilization a poor dirt road practically impassable when it rained. Mr. and Mrs. A. J. Newcomb gave us two little rooms, and we found they were alive to the value of Indian life around them in its religious aspect. They were very much devoted to Klah, a Medicine Man, grandson of Narbona, the great chief whom our soldiers killed under a flag of truce in 1847. Klah, who lived close by, had shown his kindness to the Newcombs on many occasions, coming over to protect Mrs. Newcomb from molestation when Mr. Newcomb was away, and being willing that they should see his ceremonies, as he trusted them not to interfere. At that time the Indians were much afraid of the attitude of the white people which was unsympathetic to their worship and religion.

I went with the Newcombs to a Yehbechai and met Klah, who was officiating. At that time he had begun to make his sandpainting blankets, weaving them himself, making usually one or two a year to support himself, and also to record the sandpaintings. As he said to Mr. Newcomb he knew that the Navajo boys should go to school and learn to read and to speak English, but that when they had been to school they could not remember the religious myths, sandpaintings and ritual, and so he was beginning to record them. He was teaching a nephew his Yehbechai, but had no other student to whom he could pass on his knowledge. He knew the myth of the Mountain Chant and its ritual, but did not give the ceremony. He knew the Hail Chant completely and this died with him. He also gave the Blessing Chant and the Wind Chant and knew the complete Creation Myth. I saw him later at the Newcombs and began to ask him questions about the Fire Dance which I had seen, thanks to his giving me the date of it. He asked me why I questioned him, and I said truly that I was interested in religion. I had to communicate through an interpreter always, but we were friends almost at once.

He told me some nice little stories but I felt they were superficial. Then he said he wanted me to make phonograph records of his songs, for he was a great singer as a Medicine Man must be, since almost all the ceremonies consist of songs or chants; (there are eight hundred for the Creation Myth, and four hundred and forty for the Hail Chant).

Later he came to my house at Alcalde where I had secured a recording machine and some one to run it, but there was a delay, and suddenly one day he said, "I will tell you a story if you are not afraid to take it, for the only man who has recorded one of our myths" (Matthews, twenty-five or more years ago) "was paralyzed after taking it." I said I was not afraid, and got an interpreter, and we began. Mr. Newcomb wrote and I asked questions and checked any uncertainties through the interpreter. This has been my usual technique, except that often I have done the writing. This first story was the myth of Tsilthkehje, the Mountain Chant.

You cannot hurry the story nor ask too many questions as if it has a very definite pattern, and when after eight days' work it was finished, Klah said, "tell her that every word of this is true." He told this in May when there may be thunder, and the Navajos are not supposed to tell the myths except after the first frost. Their feeling seems to be that they are releasing so much power that it is not safe when thunder is possible. Klah, being so powerful and naturally fearless, took the risk, and the reason he was afraid for me and for Arthur Newcomb was that we were unprotected; so after talking for four days he said he must go back to his home to get something to protect us, and Arthur took him back—three hundred and forty miles. When the story was finished he asked us to inhale some incense and eat some medicine-substance to protect us, and this we did. He gave me some of these two medicines which I was to take every six months.

Next Fall, when I went by invitation to a Yehbechai given by him, he watched to see if I was well, and since no harm had come to the tribe, he felt that all was well and was willing to show me more, and to tell me his other myths.

He eventually told them all to me; the Creation Myth out in Santa Barbara, for I knew that he longed to see the western ocean where Estsanah-tlehay, The Changing Woman, lives, and later he visited me in Maine so as to see the eastern sea. I grew to respect and love him for his real goodness, generosity—and holiness, for there is no other word for it. He never had married, having spent twenty-five years studying not only the ceremonies he gave, but all the medicine lore of the tribe. He helped at least eight of his nieces and nephews with money and goods. When the Newcombs first settled at Nava (as the Newcomb trading-post used to be called), half-way between Gallup and Shiprock, Klah was counted one of the rich men there with many sheep. He had his final initiation ceremony shortly after, when he reached as high rank as possible in his religion, and at that ceremony he gave away most of his goods. When I knew him he never kept anything for himself. It was hard to see him almost in rags at his ceremonies, but what was given him he seldom kept, passing it on to someone who needed it.

When a district nurse came to the day school his attitude was perfectly friendly and cooperative, and at one time when his favorite niece was bitten by a rattler while he was away, and she was treated by the nurse, he was delighted, but held a ceremony later over the niece to clear her mind of the snake fear. At another ceremony the nurse brought cough medicine and dosed Klah and the patient during the ceremony, also to his delight. He was teaching his Yehbechai ceremony to his nephew Beyal, but to Klah's great grief Beyal died about five years ago and Klah was too old to teach another nephew, for he wanted as pupil a boy of not more than six years who had never been to school, as he found that after schooling they had not the capacity to memorize the long songs, prayers and myths. Later he gave the Hail ceremony so that I could see and record it, and sang the songs for recording—there are four hundred and forty of them.

After I had recorded his great ceremonies and myths I went on to other Medicine Men and always found that when I told them of Klah and the idea of the Museum to keep the records safe for their people and mine, and of the ceremonies I had already seen, they were willing to tell their myths and show me what I needed to know. When they saw Mrs. Newcomb's sandpainting copies and found she also was really seeking for the absolutely correct version, they were anxious that their own sandpainting should be in her collection. Of course we both paid for the time occupied in working with us, as was only fair, and in the case of myths this was often a matter of many days' hard work. All the community of Nava finally became interested in helping us and took pride in the completeness of our knowledge and would show off Mrs. Newcomb's knowledge of sandpaintings to visiting Medicine Men. I admired their attitude very much; no jealousy—only a joy in finding understanding and sympathy from white people in the thing they cared for the most.

I have traveled all over the Reservation trying to get in touch with the older Medicine Men who knew the big fundamental ceremonies, for I felt, and time proves me right, that I must work as fast as possible if I was to record the old pure material. Now with school boys carrying on, the ceremonies are tending to grow shorter and simpler, and that has been happening for years—the sandpaintings grow smaller and the myth, which is the last thing to be learned by a student, is forgotten. Mrs. Newcomb and I were very lucky to have come in touch first with one of the great men of the tribe, who was not only that, but a real student of his religion. Our civilization and miracles he took simply without much wonder, as his mind was occupied with his religion and helping his people. It was wonderful to travel with him, as he knew the ceremonial names and legends of all the mountains, rivers and places, and the uses and associations of plants and stones. Everything was the outward form of the spirit world that was very real to him. He became continually more deeply interested in the idea of the recording of his religion, and showed and told me more each year. He also helped Mrs. Newcomb to make a beginning of her magnificent collection of sandpaintings by telling her when and where ceremonies were being given, and explaining her purpose to the other Medicine Men. Often he would arrange that a ceremony should be given for one of his family or clan, and Mrs. Newcomb and I were welcome, as we were sponsored by Klah, and brought appropriate gifts of tobacco or food, and sometimes I would undertake to bring the needed Medicine Man if he lived far off. Klah always knew the Medicine Men who were most respected in their form of ceremonies, and without Klah neither Mrs. Newcomb nor I could have begun nor carried on our work.

My purpose through all the work had been to establish a Museum to contain all the material we had collected, as well as all available material collected or published by others, for the use of future students of Navajo religion, art, and culture. The idea of making a building based upon the Navajo ceremonial Hogahn, as designed by the architect, Mr. Wm. P. Henderson, had Klah's strong approval from the beginning—he was frequently consulted as to details of symbolism in the permanent decorations—and he said he wanted his medicine to be kept there after his death. Klah died within the year in which the actual building was begun, but the Hogahn Beyin, House Blessing, was held as he desired by members of his family, and to me his spirit is always an inspiration to carry on what was as much his work as it is mine.

Mary C. Wheelwright.
Alcalde, New Mexico.

General Introduction

Navajo Myths

In approaching the study of this religion, two things are helpful. The first is a respect for it as one of the many great efforts of man to attempt to explain his immediate world, and to adjust himself to it and find happiness, peace and health; the second is a feeling about nature which we town-dwellers and scientifically-minded people have lost, which our remote ancestors had and children still have, of the oneness of the universe: man, animals, rain, wind, fire, the mountains and stones being all alive and being dual in their form, consisting of spirit and matter.

The myths of the Navajos are all on more or less one pattern, except the Creation Story, which is what its name implies: Hahjeenah, the Emergence. In the version that Klah gave me, Begochiddy, the Great God, and several powers, or Demigods, and a form of human being first created were living in an underworld of darkness. They climb up from world to world of increasing light, creating more forms of life until finally emerging on this world and creating Man of the substance of the whole universe. In this, Begochiddy, the Great God, is the moving and directing spirit, but is not arbitrary in his creative action, for on every occasion when something has to be decided or done, he calls a Council and acts only when there has been a discussion. He knows all that has happened and is going to happen, but takes action only when it is clear that the First Created Beings have no suggestions to offer. He shows pity for the First Creation when it is menaced by the monsters infesting this earth who threaten the First Created Beings with extinction. After the creation of Man, when the earth has been cleansed by a flood and newly furnished by him with life, and he has created the Sun and Moon and Stars and Seasons and established the habits of Men, Begochiddy goes up into heaven where he remains.

In another version of the Creation Story, Begochiddy is not an importamt force, but Man is created by the water, earth and sky; and in still another version, Man is descended from so-called First Man and First Woman, both being evil. (This is the Hanelthnayhe Myth.)

In general, the other myths began with confusion and hardship, centering round a Man who is often bad or disobedient and who, for no apparent virtue in him, is chosen by the Gods. They test his courage and enterprise by warning him of danger in certain adventures which he has the courage to attempt, or by suffering, and then he begins to learn the ceremonies so as to become the vehicle of a certain kind of healing to his own family and people. In one story he is lustful, in another a gambler, in another rash, in another disobedient, and in many myths he suffers much; and the hero, after giving his knowledge to his people, is always taken by the Gods to their home in exchange for the knowledge they have given him. Where the myth is complete it sometimes begins in an earlier world and ends with the passing on of the knowledge of the Ceremony to the people.

The Gods are not Gods in the sense of the Greeks and others, for there is no account of their characteristics or adventures apart from their relation to men, and are often personifications of Fire, Wind, Water, the Lightning and certain animals. Also, there are the twin heroes of a later part of the Creation Story, Nayenezgani and Tobachischin, who slew the monsters that were destroying Man; and also there is the bearer of seeds to Men, Beganaskiddy; Hashje-altye, the talking God and Go-between; the messenger Fly, Dontso; the great thunderbird, Iknee; the rainbow, Natseelit, that protects their sandpaintings from harmful influences; the holy people, Diginneh; and the Yeh who are beneficent spirits. Begochiddy and First Man and First Woman do not appear much in the myths, but all the other powers take part and they are often terrible. The object of the whole ritual ceremony seems to be the appeasement and control by the expert of these powers, and the achievement of the right relationship between the individual and his universe. The Navajos call this relation Hozhonji, blessing or happiness.

In the myths the forces of nature are made to take form and through this strange world the hero wanders in trouble until he is made over by the powers into a conductor of magic help to his people to heal their bodies and minds. For the ceremonies are all for cleansing from evil and sickness and bringing in the strength of the powers involved in each myth and ceremony. The hero of the story is often helped by Animal People, such as the Owl, the Squirrel, and injured by others, such as the Rock Wren, Toad and Frog (usually when he belittles their powers). The Bat and Wren are both very fearless and powerful people, the first beneficent, the second mischievous. The Coyote was one who came up from the first world and while there was the bringer of fire, but later he became uniformly mischievous in the stories. As the hero travels and suffers, he learns his medicine plants, stones, and songs, and is made into a good transmitter of power to heal. This is paralleled in the training of the Medicine Man now, for he is supposed not to learn everything from any one teacher but to go from one to another, and the myth is learned last. The thing symbolized in the myth is that Man can be made over in body and mind by belief and ritual, and that though weak and full of faults, if he shows courage and enterprise, he can be made powerful by the powers above. This is particularly definite in the Big Star myth, where various bodily signs are mentioned which are to warn men when to be still and wait for inspiration. Also, one of the heroes of the myth who has been disobedient and helpless under the punishment which follows his disobedience is able to subdue Niholtso, the Cyclone, when he has the courage to face him.

It is not a religion of fear and there is little fear in the myths. Often the chosen prophet is very lonely and shows a great curiosity, and there is much family affection and glimpses of times of starvation and much wandering about, for each Medicine Man travels in search of his knowledge. The Gods also are great wanderers. The fear of death or dying is not mentioned and the fear of the spirits of the dead, which is very strong in the people, is not spoken of in the myths. In the Creation Story, when the Sun has been created his heart will not begin to beat until someone has died, so death is necessary and not evil. Also, the Ethkaynah-ashi, the mysterious medium through which Begochiddy breathes life into creation, are twin substances created from twins which had been killed, so the breath of life has to pass through death in their creation myth, and the Ethkaynah-ashi are believed to be present mystically in every ceremony. The mountains are considered very holy as each has a spirit form as well as a material one, and the Navajos pray to them as sources of power. The great Snake is terrible and transforms men into snakes in his anger, but also may be prevailed upon to give a healing ceremony, as in the Wind and Star Chants. Even the little fire poker left behind in a deserted Hogahn speaks and tells the hero where his family has gone. Colors are full of meaning, and each time of day, like the blue before dawn, the yellow after sunset, and the noon have their special power to help and strengthen. The country where the hero of the myth wanders, or where the believing Navajo now lives, is very full of possibilities of adventure and mystery and power that he can find and use if he knows how to do so. The use of repetition in the myths and songs is for the magic purposes of the ritual and is common to all religions.

I leave to experts in psychology and ethnology the definition and analysis of these myths for I consider myself no expert, but a humble student and recorder who kept theories in the background, content to be a blank page on which has been written simply and frankly as exact a recording as a member of another race can give, for no white person can be sure that all the thoughts of an Indian are open to him. My only qualifications for the undertaking are plenty of time and patience, some knowledge of other religions and backgrounds, and a respect and love for the Navajo people.

Ceremonies

As this is, I hope, the beginning of the publication of all my material, I put the general description of ceremonies in this first volume.

These ceremonies have been recorded from personal observation except in a few cases where I had already seen parts of a ceremony, and as they are all on the same great pattern, I could be pretty sure of the ritual from description. I have recorded objectively, with no preconceived notion of what I was or was not going to see, and the interesting thing is that the same general pattern governs all the ceremonies, so that in describing the particular ceremonies, this introduction can be used for reference. Where small so-called "sings" are held and given other names, I think most of them would be found to be part of one of the major ceremonies, for in the most complete versions of the myths the different forms of ceremonies are mentioned and often described. In almost all the shorter ceremonies recorded which now last not more than five nights, the Medicine Man said that they had been nine-day ceremonies originally. All the ceremonies center around a patient, Hatrali (one sung over), who may be sick or merely sick in mind, i.e., frightened by a dream, or who may be needing only a ceremony in order to learn it in the course of being initiated into full power of officiating in that chant—for a Medicine Man cannot give a healing ceremony until he has had the ceremony given over him.

The first four days of a nine-day ceremony are called Hotchonji, having reference to cleansing from evil. First the Hogahn is blessed. This is usually a building such as the Navajos live in, though for a big ceremony a new and larger type is built especially. Then the rites for four days are for the cleansing of the patient's body by taking an emetic every morning and a sweat bath, also eating special light food, not smoking, and generally clearing the body. In the evenings a ceremony called Wohltrahd is often held which consists in the untying of knots. The ceremonies in which I have seen this Wohltrahd rite are the following: Tohe, Willachee, Nahtohe Hotchonji, Nahtohe Ba-ahd, Nahtohe Kin-be-hatral, Nilthchiji eekah thlunji, Sontsoji, Tleji (first night), Etsosi, Yohe, Hozhoni Ba-ahd, Hozhoni Baka, and Mah-ih. Another form consists of the cutting of wreaths of spruce twigs which are woven into Yucca strings and twined and tied all over the patient's body. This is called the Trohgish rite. Both of these rites may symbolize liberating or untying trouble in the mind. On the fourth night they sometimes hold the Oody Klahd rite, when the patient, protected by a sandpainting, is frightened by someone dressed as the Bear or a Wild Man—the appearance in bodily form of fear. If the patient faints, a ceremony called Hashtehl-neh is held to restore him. This I have seen in Etsosi, Tsilthkehji Ba-ahd, Tsilthkehij Baka, Nahtohe Kin-behatral, Hozhoni Ba-ahd, and Tleji (fourth night).

During the first four days the Tsepanse ceremony may also be held. In this ceremony each day big hoops are made of thin sticks about three feet long, tied butt to tip with yucca cord holding spruce twigs or holy plants in bunches. The hoops are set up in a line outside and east of the Hogahn on the first day to the south of it on the second, to the west on the third, and north on the fourth day. Through these the patient passes while a cloth or skin is slowly removed from over his bead and body, thereby typifying the shedding of his old personality. This happens in the Hanelthnayhe, Sontso Hotchonji, Nilthchiji Ba-ahd Hotchonji, Nahtohe Hotchonji, Willachee, Yohe (in connection with bath outdoors during the first four days of ceremony), and the Tohe Hotchonji (first four days).

When the patient and his family have talked over whether they can afford the food which has to be provided for the Medicine Man and his helper, and the men who make the sandpaintings, and the fee for the Medicine Man, they decide which one to call in and send for him. When he arrives, the near relatives of the patient collect the colored sandstones to be ground for sandpaintings and the special herbs the Medicine Man needs, practically always the four holy plants, Giss-dil-yessi, Toh-ih-kath, Tsay zhee, and Dlah-nastrasseh, and some others. He brings with him his feather and prayer wands, rattles, pollen and material for the reed and stick Kehtahns and the paint for them, feathers and crystal, jet, abalone and white shell, powdered incense often made of bird feathers and herbs, and whatever else is needed to put into and with the Kehtahns. The Medicine Man brings vessels to hold the infusions of herbs, the rattles to accompany the singing and usually a helper who knows the songs and sandpaintings. The Kehtahns are made by someone who has some knowledge of the ceremonies, under the direction of the Medicine Man. This applies also to the sandpaintings, which usually require six or eight painters working at once under direction. These are not necessarily experts, for quite young boys often help.

The pattern of the ceremonies is similar in all of them except the Anadji, beginning with a collection of medicines, the preparation of four pokers for the fire, usually made of oak. On the first night often they only sing songs accompanied by the rattles, and when they begin to sing an assistant goes outside and whirls the Chindi-neh (devil-chaser), a form of bull-roarer such as is used in Australia, a knife-shaped piece of wood with a cord of leather tied to its center, which the assistant whirls rapidly round his head, making a whirring sound, while encircling the Hogahn four times. The patient is always present during the singing and drinks an infusion of herbs at the end and inhales incense. In three cases that I have seen, the Tohe, Willachee, and Hozhoni Baka, there were more elaborate short ceremonies on the first night.

Early next morning the ceremonial fire is made by twirling a sharp hard stick in a hole bored in a piece of soft wood resting on shredded cedar-bark. When the bark has ignited, the big fire is lighted and burned up very hot, and water is put on to heat for the emetic infusion of herbs. Pollen is sprinkled on the ends of the four pokers for blessing and these are thrust into the fire and then withdrawn. Four twigs with oak leaves on them are stuck in between the logs of the roof to the east, south, west and north, and a little pollen is sprinkled on them. All this ritual is common to all ceremonies, pollen being the Navajo form of blessing and a silent prayer being said by the Medicine Man always as he sprinkles it.

In some ceremonies, the Sontso (Big Star), Tsilthkehji Nahtohe (Shooting Chant combined with Mountain Chant), Nilthchiji Ba-ahd eekah thlunji (Wind Chant, female, many sandpaintings), also Nilthchiji Baka (male Wind Chant), N'Dlohe (Hail Chant), Hanelthnayhe (Emergence), Hozhoni Ba-ahd (Beauty Chant, female), some sandpaintings are made for the emetic and sweating ceremony. Often these represent the symbol of the Sun or Moon surrounded by a rainbow on which the basket is placed into which the patient vomits. Rainbow spots are made on which the patient kneels and places his hands; and in others, snake paintings are made. Everything goes by fours in ceremonies and myths, cardinal points always being mentioned, also the colors connected with them, and these vary a little depending upon the ceremony, for though white for the east, blue for the south, yellow for the west, and black for the north are the most usual colors, they are not invariable.

The ceremony of making Kehtahns is always similar and is well described in Washington Matthew's *NIGHT CHANT*. A blanket is always spread west of the central fire with pieces of cotton cloth (probably they used to have corn husks) laid in a line on the blanket, and on these are placed the particular type of offering for each ceremony; usually eagle breath feathers (soft downy ones), bluebird feathers, yellow bird, small turkey feathers, tiny bits of turquoise, jet, white shell and abalone, and a bit of soft cotton cord, and often a bit of wool. The Kehtahns are made of sections of reed usually cut into three-inch lengths with a stone knife. Sometimes they are only two inches long, and sometimes up to six inches long. They are held on thin twigs thrust through them while they are being painted. This is done by the assistant who moistens the white, blue, yellow, red and black earth paints with water on some flat stones. Then he decorates the Kehtahns according to the Medicine Man's directions, using a small flat stick instead of a brush. Then he inserts a plug of bluebird-down and pushes it well into the Kehtahn with the end of an owl or woodpecker feather, then puts the offerings in, often of turquoise, jet, white shell and abalone and native tobacco. The patient is then given a crystal or a crystal-shaped piece of glass and holds this up toward the sun to catch a ray of light, then touches each filled Kehtahn with it. (Crystal is used as a symbol of truth, a Medicine Man's lips being touched with it, and it is put in the patient's shoes at the end of certain ceremonies.) The assistant moistens his finger and puts some wet yellow pollen from the tiny skin bag which contained the crystal on the top of each Kehtahn, and so seals them after the patient has touched each with the crystal. Out of this same tiny skin bag the assistant takes a little brush. The Kehtahns are placed on the pieces of cotton, and the patient dips the brush in water and strokes the Kehtahns from west to east. The Medicine Man sprinkles pollen on them and folds the cloth round each offering of Kehtahn, feathers, etc. Then, holding his bag of pollen, he takes a pinch of it and touches his forehead and tongue and throws some up to the sun four times, praying, then takes up the bundle of offerings and goes and sits close to the patient, facing him, and crouching, with left knee under him and right knee up. He touches the patient's head and tongue with pollen and then he begins the prayers to the Powers to whom the Kehtahns are offered while the patient holds the bundles in his hands. The Medicine Man says a phrase and the patient repeats it as fast as can be spoken, and the prayer often lasts a quarter of an hour. All this ritual is invariable as far as I know, though the designs on the Kehtahns and the Powers to which they are offered vary of course.

When the prayer is finished, the Medicine Man gives the bundle of offerings to an assistant, telling him to leave them for the Powers out on the surrounding country, and the assistant blesses himself with pollen, presses the bundles to the patient's feet and knees and shoulders, head, breast and back, then goes out, taking pollen with him, to sprinkle on the offerings when he leaves them. Afterwards, he brings back the pieces of cotton cloth to the Medicine Man. If they are giving a five-day ceremony, the sandpainting is begun at once, after the Kehtahn rite, but if it is a nine-day ceremony, the afternoon is spent in resting.

After dark usually the Wohltrahd Rite is held. The Medicine Man has brought with him some long eagle wing feathers, or the assistant has collected some holy plants, and he divides these into five bundles. The Medicine Man sings, with his rattle accompaniment, and the assistant ties a yard-long woolen cord ending in little prayer feathers in a lot of slip knots round each bundle of feathers or plants, depending on form of ceremony. When the bundles are ready (and the number of the bundles increases with each night of the rite, five on the first, seven on the second, nine on the third, etc., and there is usually an uneven number) the Medicine Man takes up a bundle and presses it to the patient's right foot, singing as he does it, and pulling the slip-knotted cord loose at the same time. He then takes another bundle and does the same on the other foot, then on the knees, thighs, breast, back, hands, shoulders, head and mouth. When this is finished, he takes up all the cords together and draws them from one hand to the other over these different parts of the patient's body and sometimes waves the feathers round and over the patient's head. The patient drinks an infusion of herbs and inhales some incense and the rite is over. The details vary but the form is always similar.

The body painting at night I have seen only in the Star Chant. It was on the fourth night and ended the ceremony of Hotchonji as they sang all night, which always happens at the end of any ceremony, even a short one. The fact of a night's wakefulness is most important for the patient's healing.

Sandpaintings

Navajo ritual paintings, according to some of the older myths, were originally made on buckskin and "unrolled" the ceremony. Later, it is thought, when the Navajos became more harassed by other Indians and white people, they memorized them for safety so that no one could steal their "power." It has been suggested that the Navajos got the idea of sandpainting from the Hopis and other Pueblo people who have always made patterns in sand or colored corn-meal in front of their altars in the Kivas. The art of sandpainting is, however, very old. Today the aborigines in Australia make patterns in sand, and the Mandalas of Tibet are allied in method and conception, but no race has carried the art of sandpainting so far as the Navajos.

The skill and speed with which experts can make curved figures and exquisite feathers with very delicate lines, or broad-spread masses of smooth color, is amazing, and requires not only skill but great concentration, which in itself keeps the painter's mind on the subject and thereby stamps the painting in his memory. This, I am sure, is partly what they are for, to imprint on the minds of the younger men the images of the gods, for the sandpaintings are a sort of shorthand way to remember the myths. This is not their principal meaning, however, for the pattern of the ceremonies mentioned above in *Introduction to Ceremonies* is four days of cleansing the body and mind, and then the materialization of the Gods and Powers concerned with each ceremony. They are portrayed in sand, then hallowed, and then used in healing and strengthening the patient by the actual touch of the parts of the sandpainting to the body of the patient, and by his drinking of an infusion in which the sand of the painting has been placed, whereby the patient is in contact with the painting externally and internally.

They are certainly a form of art, not used for self expression but to bring before men the Powers in visible stylized form, abstract and very powerful, even to an outsider, in the suggestion of splendid symbols for very abstract ideas. They are destroyed through their use as connecting links between Gods and men, for only in the short space of time after the last painter has finished his work, and the time when the priest walks sunwise onto the painting and puts pollen and white corn meal on it, can it be seen completed and untouched. After this the patient and other members of his family sprinkle it with white meal and the patient sits down on it facing east, and the treatment begins.

The Ceremonial Hogahn always faces east, in fact most Navajo houses do so, and when the sandpainting is to be begun the fire is moved from the center to just in front of the door. Then smooth sand is spread all over the floor and the painting is begun in the center, usually by the Medicine Man. The straight lines are made by snapping a string between two painters across the painting, and the batten used in weaving is used to smooth the sand. Errors are covered with fresh sand and good humor prevails—I've never seen anyone made fun of for a mistake except in a friendly way.

From the east comes the Sun, thus it is the most propitious direction, so when the picture is finished the heads of the figures are eastward, unless they are made radiating from a center; and the whole picture is usually surrounded by a rainbow figure, Natseelit, with her head and hands to the northeast and her feet to the southeast, and a wide space between her head and feet.

This rainbow is to protect the painting from evil influences which might come to it from the south, west, and north, and the eastern opening are often two guardian figures to protect it, often Dontso, the Messenger fly, Jahbunny the Bat, the Bear (in Mountain Chant), sometimes Sun and Moon. If the painting is very full of power it does not have the surrounding protection, and in some ceremonies of great power lightning and snakes are used. Sometimes the deities stand on a black bar which typifies the earth below the horizon or a cave. This is on the west of the sandpainting and on each end of it is often a bar of chequer pattern edging the sandpainting north and south and ending in bundles of feathers; this is a rope of braided rain.

The faces of the figures are always masked, and the masks are white or blue, or brown or black, or all four colors, but black only in the case of the

Fire-Gods. The chin of the faces is always colored yellow for pollen and their necks are always blue with four red stripes for protection, for the rainbow colors red and blue are for this purpose. The hands of the figures are always white, except in the Wind Chant, and in any ceremonial dance now the hands of the dancers are whitened. From the arms hang medicine bundles on long strings of Shah-bekloth, ray of light or rainbow, the red colors always on the outside and the blue next the body of the figure. Sometimes the strings are of skin, otter, weasel, etc. The heads are usually square for female figures and round for male, but this is not invariable. The colors on the bodies and the colors edging them usually are blue edged with yellow, or yellow edged with blue for females; black edged with white or white edged with black for males. The white figures are placed to the east, blue to the south, yellow to the west, and black to the north. But in several paintings the east is black and north is white and this changes all the sequences.

The rainbow colors are always separated by white lines and edged with white and in general these combinations mentioned hold good. South and west are feminine, and north and east masculine.

The kilts on the figures are red in the Mountain Chant, but in other Chants are usually white with a pattern-like embroidery, and tassels at corners. The pouch at the waist can be made according to the fancy of the painter, the only thing on which he can use his own design; the rest is absolutely rigid in the ritual symbolism.

The central motif in the paintings which radiate from a center, is usually water surrounded by the four colors. They set a little bowl in the sand and the Medicine Man fills it with water and then sprinkles it thick with black powdered charcoal on which he often makes two or four short rainbow bars. It typifies pure water. Sometimes cloud symbols or dragon-flies surround it. From the four corner directions, northeast, southeast, southwest and northwest grow out the four holy plants, corn, beans, squash and tobacco, always painted in the same way, with three white roots going to the central black water under the earth. Sometimes the central figure, when square, means a house. The masked deities, often eight in number, which stand on east, south, west and north of the center, have below their feet Shah-bekloth, ray-of-light bars, and little rainbow spots also are often placed on their bodies for protection. In their hands they hold fir twigs, or rattles or bows and arrows, or little magic baskets in which they can be transported from one place to another. They are usually characters in the myth, or wind or thunder people or people of the corn.

Sometimes there are snakes in various forms, as in Wind Chant, or in Hozhoni and Nahtohe, and when portrayed in animal form the bodies of the snakes always zigzag in four angles, and usually have an oblong symbol which is a house, painted figures which are deer tracks, and two half moons interlocking like the Chinese symbols of Yin and Yang on their bodies. Sometimes the animals, such as snake or buffalo, are in human form. They are not baleful, merely powerful, and almost every series of sandpaintings includes a snake or animal painting, a painting showing sky elements, and one to do with the plants.

Sometimes the first sandpainting will be of snakes, the second thunder, the next plants, and the last one of an abstraction, like the whole sky, or arrows of power, or one which includes both water and sky.

The figures sometimes have spines projecting from them and these mean that the Powers are in armor of "Bezh" which is apparently flint and these warriors usually hold arrows in their hands.

Etsan-ah-tlehay, the Changing Woman (possibly Nature who was born of earth and sky when Begochiddy took pity on man and created her to be the mother of Nayenezgani and Tobachischin who killed the monsters), never appears in sandpaintings, nor Begochiddy nor any of those who were in the first world, except Hashjeshjin, the Fire-god; Hashje-altye, the Talking god, who is much in the Tleji or Yehbechai; Hashje-Hogahn; Beganaskiddy; Dontso, the Fly; Jahbunny, the Bat; Wuzzy Kitty, the caterpillar; the Sun, Moon, Stars, Bear, Buffalo; the Great Thunderbird, Iknee; Winds; and the Holy People, Deginnih. The Yehs (gods) and Eagle people appear often.

The bear, deer, antelope, mountain sheep, otter, badger, etc., usually have a line from their mouths to their hearts which is their breath. The birds are shown in fairly life-like form and the blue-bird often is a symbol for happiness. The direction in which the figures are supposed to be moving, which is always from left to right, sunwise, is shown by the legs and direction of the feathers on heads, for the figures are always front face, and they often wear necklaces or collars of fur and beads; and the arms and wrists are protected by rainbow marks. On their heads are ritual feathers, usually eagle and turkey plumes, a small turquoise is in the middle of the forehead, and often on each side and above the face is a red line enclosed in two black lines. This typifies hair enclosing a line of life and is tied at intervals with white cord. Sometimes very elaborate head-dresses and medicine bundles which look like arrows are used, as in Mountain Chant.

Sandpainting Ritual

The actual sandpainting is made by relations or friends of the patient under the direction of the Medicine Man. Assistants carry into the Hogahn fresh sand and spread it evenly over most of the floor space. Then pieces of white, red, and rellow sandstone are brought in and ground on a large flat stone with a smaller stone by an assistant. For the black color, charcoal is used mixed with enough sand to make it pour easily; the blue color is made by a mixture of charcoal and the white sand. The actual painting is made by each painter taking a little sand and pouring it out on the background through the thumb and the nearly closed joint of the right hand index finger. Great skill is shown by the experts who can make a line as fast as a person can draw with a brush. They are able to make a fine or broad line or spread a background color by changing the position of the fingers. They sit, or kneel, and have to concentrate absolutely to do their work well, which fixes the images they draw thoroughly in their minds, so that the first thing the young men learn, and that they all enjoy, is the making of the paintings. Cotton string, held between two men at opposite sides, is used to snap on the sand to mark straight lines, and the batten for weaving is used to smooth the foundation sand. The central portion of the design is always made first and spreads outward, the number of painters often increasing as the sandpainting grows larger.

It is interesting to note that the Mandalas made in Tibet in rice powder, and copied in paint by the Chinese, Japanese, and East Indians, are similar in religious purpose to the Navajo sandpaintings. The aborigines of Australia also make sandpaintings for ritual use. Among the Hopi and Rio Grande Pueblos, patterns made in corn meal before the Kiva altars also have ritual significance.

When the sandpainting is finished, the prayer sticks are set up around outside the encircling figure, and the particular ceremonial tablets called n'Dee-ah which are used in the ceremony are set up side by side west of the sandpainting. The tablets are oblong, made of thin wood, with a tapered spike at the bottom to stick into the earth. They are about four inches high by three broad, and painted with symbols on both sides. Every morning before dawn the tablets are taken out and stuck in the altar in front of the door outside and only brought into the Hogahn when the sandpainting is finished. These tablets are used in Nahtohe (Shooting Chant), Ba-ahd and Baka, N'Dlohe (Hail Chant), Tohe (Water Chant), Nilthchiji (Wind Chant), Sontsoji (Big Star Chant), and Hozhoni (Beauty Chant).

After the placing of the tablets, several bowls of infusions of herbs are filled and placed in or near the hands on the north end of the encircling rainbow figure. At the other, south, end are placed plumed arm bundles, the Medicine Man's necklaces of fur with whistles fastened to it, and any other feathered medicine bundles.

The patient often is ceremonially bathed on the morning when the sandpaintings begin, the sixth day in a nine-day ceremony, the second in a five-day ceremony, such as Tohe; but in many ceremonies, the Willachee, Nilthchiji-eekah-thlunji, Nahtohe Baka, for instance, the ceremonial bath is given just before the painting of the body on the last day of the ceremony. This ceremony is always similar, with the making of a symbol in pollen on the sand, then placing a mat of fir boughs and on this a well washed basket filled with water and a piece of amole, soap weed. The Medicine Man sprinkles pollen on this and makes a suds and the patient bathes his whole body, hair, and even his necklaces in the water and puts on new clothes if possible. If the patient is a woman, other women hold up blankets to hide her. The Medicine Man touches the patient's body, limbs and head with white meal and then the patient rubs it all over his body and clothing, and the Medicine Man blesses him with pollen.

When an altar is made outside the door during the days of sandpaintings in the Hogahn, this is always set up before light in the morning, at night the mound is left protected by boards or brush, and the plumed wands and tablets are replaced before daylight each day and when the sandpainting is ready are brought in and used around it as described. This outside altar is known as the Dawn Altar.

The rite of hallowing the sandpainting begins with the placing by the Medicine Man of pollen on the heads, feet, hands, medicine bundles and all important places in the painting. Then his assistant puts pinches of white cornmeal on these same places and dips the asperger, which is a wand wound with different colors and ending in a feather or fur, in the liquid infusion and touches these piles of white meal with it, continually dipping it in the liquid, thereby putting some of the meal and sandpainting into the infusion. He must not step on the figures in the sandpainting and must enter at the open east side and circle from south to north, sunwise; meantime the Medicine Man and others are singing, accompanied by rattles. Then the patient is called in and sprinkles the painting with white cornmeal under the direction of the Medicine Man, and sits south of the door and takes off his clothes. The assistant then collects the little piles of corn-meal and puts the meal aside.

The patient is told where to sit on the sandpainting, facing east, and many songs are sung. The Medicine Man goes on the sandpainting, often erasing guardian symbols as he does so, and stirring up infusion, gives patient to drink of it four times, motioning as he does so as if it came from above. Then moistening his hands with the infusion, he presses his hands to the vital points of the painting, feet, knees, hands, shoulders, reast, back and head, each time afterwards pressing his hands to the same parts of the patient's body, feet to feet, hands to hands, etc. Then he gives him the infusion to drink again, four times, and some to rub on his body. Then the assistant puts live coals from the fire in front of him, and the Medicine Man sprinkles incense powder on them, making a smoke, and the patient inhales it and rubs it over his body, then leaves the Hogahn.

When there is to be a painting of the patient's body, the rite begins in the same way except that a pellet called Ahyehl, which contains every kind of holy substance connected with the particular ceremony, is placed on the sandpainting and given to the patient to complete the cure, and the Medicine Man presses his medicine bundles and the tablets to all the vital centers of the patient's body, beginning with the soles of the feet, and on up to the head. He presses his own foot to the patient's foot with medicine bundle between, his head to patient's head, shoulder to shoulder, and so forth; then twists the patient's body, holding his medicine bundles to breast and back. This is called Atsis and usually comes after the giving of the Ahyehl pellet.

In certain ceremonies during the last sandpainting, cinctures are used called Tyelth. These are made of bull rush strings braided with spruce or holy plants woven into them, and consist of bracelets and two wreaths long enough to go over the head and under one arm, so they cross on the breast and back. They are first put on and worn by the Medicine Man as he begins to treat the patient, and then transferred to the patient when the treatment is nearly finished. They represent jewelry ritually, and are worn by the patient all the following night, and the next morning are taken out and left in a wood. On the last day of treatment, the patient is given a new name, and a small prayer plume with a bit of turquoise and white shell is tied to his hair. When the patient is a woman, the shell should be abalone.

The painting of the patient's body takes place before the treatment on the last sandpainting, while the patient sits north of the sandpainting. The Medicine Man usually touches the patient's body with infusion, indicating shape and kind of symbolic design to be made. His assistant then does the painting, using moistened earth paint and little flat sticks for paint brushes. When the patient is ready, he is led on to the sandpainting by the Medicine Man with the asperger or prayer stick. The treatment is as usual, but includes taking of the Ahyehl pellet and subsequent Atsis rite, and tying on of head and arm plumes, after which the Medicine Man often whistles at each ear and carries the sound on up toward the sky. The patient then inhales incense and is led off the sandpainting by the Medicine Man, while the assistant sprinkles water before the patient as he goes out the door.

The Medicine Man erases the sandpainting each day with the asperger or plumed wand, and the sand is taken out and deposited in a desert place. On the last day, after the sandpainting is destroyed, they spread a blanket and bring in a basket of cornmeal and place it in the center of the Hogahn. The Medicine Man puts a cross and circle of pollen on it and the patient is called in and after songs are sung is fed mush by the Medicine Man from east, south, west, and north sides of the basket, and then the Medicine Man and patient finish it. Singing goes on all through the treatment on the sandpainting.

Another rite that should be mentioned is the initiation in the Tleji (Yehbe-chai). I've seen it in the evening in the Medicine Hogahn on the fifth night and think it took place probably on last four nights, but it usually happens on the last afternoon of the ninth day. The boys and girls to be initiated go out beyond the dancing ground, east of the Hogahn, and sit down in a line facing east, hiding their faces in blankets over their heads. The boys are naked, except for G-string, the girls dressed. The Gods Hashje-altye and Hashje-hogahn, wearing their traditional masks, appear coming from the East. Hashje-altye goes to the boys and gives his call, Yo-ho-ho-ho, and lightly whips each one with yucca leaves, while Hashje-hogahn gives his call and presses two corn ears to the girls' heads. The children mustn't look up. Then the two gods unmask and lay the masks down before the children, and the children are told to look up. The men put the masks in front of the children's faces so that they look through them, and then the masks are laid on the ground and each child in turn goes up to the masks and puts pollen on them.

The Story of the Emergence - *Hahdenigai-Hunai*

First World

The story starts in the Running-Pitch place or Jah-dokonth. Hashjeshjin, the son of the Fire, whose mother is a Comet, and Etsay-Hasteen, the first man, who is the son of Night and whose father is Nah-doklizh, which is the blue above the place where the Sun has set, were there; also Estsa-assun, who is the first woman, whose mother is the Daybreak and whose father is Nahtsoi which is the yellow light after the Sun has set; also Etsay-hashkeh or Coyote Man, whose mother is Yah-zheh-kih, or the Dawn Light. The fifth who is there is Begochiddy, the blue-eyed and yellow-haired god, the great god, whose mother is a Ray of Sunlight, Shah-bekloth, and whose father is the Daylight, Shun-deen; also Asheen-assun, the Salt Woman whose mother was Tohe-estan, or Water Woman, and whose father was Tsilth-tsa-assun, or Mountain Man. (He looks like a woman but is a man.) These are the six people who were living on the dark earth or first world, Jah-dokonth.

On the dark earth Begochiddy built in the east a white mountain; in the south a blue mountain, in the west a yellow mountain, and in the north a black mountain, and he also made mountains surrounding all the dark earth and the colored mountains, and these were called Tsilth-nah-n' deel-doi, which means colored mountains which appear and disappear; and in the center of the world Begochiddy made a red mountain.

He also created the red ants, Willachee, and the black ants, Willazhini, which run in a line on the logs in the mountains, the yellow ants, Willa-klitsoi, and wood ants, Willachee-tsai, which are half red and half black, also Nicky-dol-zholi or gray ants. He named them as they were created and smiled as he made them. He also made Nahasan-b' hogahndi, which lives in the ground, and Wolazhi, which is a tiny black ant, also Neho-neh-yahni, or "black bug which flies around", and which is the Midge.

On the east side under the mountains he planted some bamboo, or Lukatso. On the south side he planted big sunflowers, N'd'gilly-tso. On the west side under the mountains he planted Luka, or reed. On the north side under the mountains he planted small sunflowers, N'd'gilly.

After Begochiddy had created these things he gave them Tsa-tlai (First Law). In the first world there was one law, in the second two laws, in the third three laws, and in the fourth four laws.

Begochiddy now created Kay-des-tizhi (Wound in a Rainbow), who is both man and woman. By this time the ants that he had created had increased very much.

Hashjeshjin asked Begochiddy why there should be only one law and why he, Hashjeshjin, should not be able to make some laws. Begochiddy answered: "I made the law, and there shall be no other." So Hashjeshjin grew angry and said: "Just because you have made the ants and man, you think you are very great and for that reason I will burn the things you have made and the world, too." And four days later Hashjeshjin started burning the world.

Begochiddy told the first man, Etsay-Hasteen, to go to the east mountain and get some earth and some of the Lukatso plants and bring them back to him, and he told Estsa-assun, the first woman, to go to the south mountain and bring him some of the big sunflowers, N'd'gilly-tso, and Etsay Hasteen also went to the west mountain and brought back earth and Luka (reed plants), and Estsa-assun also went to the north mountain and brought earth and small sunflowers, N'd'gilly. [1]

In the center of the red mountain Begochiddy stuck the Lukatso, the big bamboo, and all of the creatures that he had created entered into it. The bamboo now started to grow with all that were in it, growing higher and higher until it reached the second world, the blue world, Naho-doklizh-dasakah, overhead, and grew into it. The little tiny black ants came out first into the new world and after them the rest of the ants and then the people, and next to the last came Etsay-hashkeh, and last of all Hashjeshjin. When all had climbed out of the bamboo, Begochiddy pulled the bamboo up into the second world and Hashjeshjin blew into the hole four times which made the hole close up and the first world burned up and is still burning.

Second World

Begochiddy took the earth brought from the first world and created mountains in the east, south, west, and north, and plants similar to those in the first world, and he planted white cotton in the east, blue cotton in the south, yellow cotton in the west, and black cotton in the north. On this world the soil was not rich enough to plant crops. He created the humble bee, honey bee, yellow jacket, and the black wasp. He made twin men and twin women and Begochiddy smiled as he created all these things.

Hashjeshjin did not like this world or the creatures there and told Begochiddy that he wanted to kill the male twins and Begochiddy answered: "Why not kill both the male and female twins?" Hashjeshjin answered him twice in the same way and then he killed the twins. So Begochiddy had made two laws.

Then Begochiddy slit the bodies of the male twins from the neck down to the legs, and cut the flesh into small pieces, and cut off the ends of the fingers and toes and put all the pieces back into the heads. He then did the same to the female twins, starting at the feet and cutting upwards, and the pieces he put into their heads as in the male twins. Both the male and female twins were called Ethkay-nah-ashi. He put the Lukatso (bamboo) into the male and female bodies from the head to the legs and he put a small bamboo across the mouths of the male twins, a large sunflower on the right-hand side of the face, a big bamboo across the forehead and on the left side another sunflower. On the heads of the female twins he put a reed across the chin and forehead and a small sunflower on each cheek.

Begochiddy then took a piece of bamboo a foot long and put it into the mouth of the male twins and held the other end in his mouth and then he breathed his spirit into the dead male twins and a great sound began in their bodies. And while this sound went on, in the east near the mountains the white cotton began to move, and in the south the blue cotton moved, and in the west the yellow cotton, and in the north the black cotton, and then all the cotton rose and changed into clouds. The white cotton turned into white clouds, the yellow to yellow clouds, the blue to blue clouds, and the black to black clouds. Begochiddy breathed into the bodies of the female twins and when the great sound began in their bodies, then under the white cloud in the east grew up Kloh-lachee, the red grass. In the south under the blue cloud grew the small yellow rabbit bush, Giss-dil-yessi. In the west under the yellow cloud grew the Tsay-zhee or gramma grass. And in the north under the black cloud grew Tohikath, the Water-Bearer. After these clouds and plants were made, the rain began in the east and went around the world in all directions.

When it had rained and the plants had flowered it made everyone very happy. They went out to the mountains and picked the flowers and smelled of them and wanted to go and live near the mountains so as to be close to the plants, but Begochiddy and Hashjeshjin said: "No, you may go up to the mountains but you must not live there." The people asked this four times and were refused each time. Hashjeshjin said: "As you are not willing to obey, I will burn the water."

Now Begochiddy created a red mountain, Yoh-lachee, a bad mountain, which gives people sores on their bodies; and he stuck the big bamboo into the top of this mountain and sent Etsay-Hasteen to gather from the east, south, west and north, all the things that had been created. And Etsay-Hasteen brought earth from the mountains and plants and clouds and put them into the big bamboo. Kay-des-tizhi, the man wrapped in the Rainbow, put the Ethkay-nah-ashi under his rainbow robe and they all went into the big bamboo while Hashjeshjin began to burn the water (oil) in the second world. [2]

Third World

The little black ants were the first to come out of the bamboo into the third world which is the yellow world, Nah-klitsoi-dasahkah. And after all were out of the bamboo, Begochiddy pulled it up into the new world and Hashjeshjin blew into the hole and closed it up. All the plants, mountains and clouds that were in the second world were planted in the third world and Begochiddy created a mountain in the center of this world called Tsilth-tla-del-tai. And he made another mountain Tsilth-n'del-tai, the second mountain, and Tsilth-tah-del-tai, the third mountain, and Tsilth-teen-del-tai the fourth mountain. Then he made Tohe-egleen, or Water Meeting Place, and then To-he-nostleh, or Crossing Waters, and in the middle of these crossing waters he put Sis-tahilth-lachee, or Red Mountain Turtle. One of these streams ran from west to east and one from north to south. [3] In the east part of the Crossing Waters he placed Tahilth-lachee, a big turtle which was red in color. In the south water he placed the red thunder, Iknee-lachee. In the west water he placed Tabasteen-lachee, red otter, and in the north water Teoltsodi-lachee, red water monster. Begochiddy then made a quick-sandy spring called Na-hodoh-othle, and a place called Lukatso-sakah, meaning the Growing Place of bamboo. Then Begochiddy made Tsilth-lakai, White Mountain (near Tellu-ride, Colorado), and he placed a white thunder bird on the top of this moun-tain and he made four cyclones, black, blue, yellow and white, and hail of four colors and put them inside of the White Mountain. He took the bamboo and breathed into the Ethkaynah-ashi and life came into the mountains, water, and animals that he had created.

Hashjeshjin created the crow, Gahgi, and the magpie, Ea-ah-ee. And Be-gochiddy made the humming bird, Data-tehe, and the turtle-dove, Hospiddy. And then through the Ethkay-nah-ashi he breathed life into the birds and gave them voices.

He made trees, and he made all kinds of animals, birds, bugs, fishes, worms, and everything. He appointed the wolf and mountain lion kings of the animals, and the oriole and mocking bird as kings of the birds, and Begochid-dy smiled as he made these animals and birds.

Begochiddy now created the first man, Etsay-Hasleen (Made Now), and Atrahgeh-Hasleen (Center Man), next Adahgeh-Hasleen (Behind Man), next Hlakah-kestrah-Hasleen (Fourth Man). And then he made four women of the same names. Kay-des-tizhi, Wound-in-a-Rainbow, took charge of all created animals, birds, and human beings, which were all created pairs. Begochiddy now created corn of four varieties, black, white, blue and yellow. Then he took the bamboo and breathed through the Ethkaynah-ashi and gave life to all that he had created. And all created life had one language which all spoke and understood. There was no Sun or Moon in this world but the mountains gave plenty of light.

Begochiddy now made himself a Rainbow house, and he and the five gods of the first world were all living under the east mountain, while the people and animals were living together in the middle of the world. The Navajos were there from the beginning and Begochiddy now made the Hopis and the Zunis. The males were made first and the females afterwards, and he made for the Zunis four gods, one, the tall god called Yeh-nez, and the other three gods called Yehs. He made the Taos (Tohwulth) Indians and gave them a male bamboo which they had to watch over, and gave the Hopi a female bamboo which they were to guard.

The six gods living under the east mountain wanted the Hopis and Navajos to be friends so they gave a female Ethkaynah-ashi to the Hopis and a male to the Navajos. By now all the Indians living together made a large group, and Begochiddy was chief of them all, and Etsay-hashkeh, Coyote Man, watched over the Indians and told the six gods how the people were getting on.

The Indians now planted four kinds of corn and Estsan-natah, Head Woman, told them what to do, and how to grind corn. By this time they had different kinds of dresses, some white and some striped with colors, and shoes made of white deer hide. They began to grow tobacco, beans, pumpkins, squash; and they planted Bezh-l'entklizi, a red flower which they needed for their eagle ceremony. All the Indians worked together in harmony. They killed the animals, mostly deer, for meat.

Now the first marriage took place, Etsay-Hasleen with Eekai-etahdeh, who was the daughter of Estsan-nahtah, Head Woman. Eekai-etahdeh liked to go down to the river and sit there most of the day. Her husband had the post of Chief-in-the-Morning, and told the people when to go hunting and before each hunt called a meeting in his Rainbow Hogahn and gave them tobacco to smoke. The door of this hogahn was made of woven reeds and was a very fine door. Etsay-Hasleen went hunting four days in succession, and each day after he had departed Eekai-etahdeh went to the river. When Etsay-Hasleen came back at night, he found his supper not ready and his wife not there. This made Etsay-Hasleen very angry, and he became jealous. On the fourth day he slipped away from his men instead of going hunting, and went down to the river and hid in the bushes where he could watch his wife. (Begochiddy and Hashjeshjin had sent a spirit to appear before the girl and make love to her but she knew nothing of this). As Etsay-Hasleen was watching, he saw something swimming towards his wife. It looked like a big bunch of weeds, but as it neared the girl the husband saw it was a handsome young man, Sethkinh. Though he looked like a man, he was really the Water Horse, Kahilth-klee, and he had put a lot of weeds on his head to conceal him in swimming. The young man and girl talked a while and the husband became very jealous and went home into his Rainbow house and laid down thinking of his wife, and he did not even smoke.

When the girl thought it time for her husband to have returned from the hunt, she went home and found him there and said to him: "When did you get back from the hunt?" and he did not answer. She asked him four times with no answer, and she then cooked some supper and served it in a very finely made basket. She was angry at his not answering her question and she told him so. The husband then said: "I am angry, too, at the way you have behaved," and pushed the food away with his foot. So his wife understood that he knew what she had been doing and she got up and ran off to her mother. She told her mother everything, and that her husband was angry with her, and her mother grew very angry and said: "Your husband is not supporting you properly although he has plenty of meat and corn and is rich." The mother ran over to the Rainbow Hogahn and sat down outside the door. And while she sat there, she scolded her son-in-law very harshly and then she went back to her own home. [4]

Etsay-Hasleen did not answer her, but got up and went to another hogahn which belonged to Kay-des-tizhi who was rich and had plenty of food and things. Etsay-Hasleen called the three other chiefs together and made them a speech, telling them about his wife and his mother-in-law, and saying that he thought they should all resign from being chiefs as they could not keep order, and they decided to do as he said.

Begochiddy knew all about this trouble and he and the five gods came to Kay-des-tizhi's hogahn and called the head people and the chiefs of the birds and animals to come to a Council. So they all came and went into the hogahn and Begochiddy said to them: "I am going to separate the men and the women, and the female birds and animals. All the males are to go and live across the river, and the females are to stay on this side of the river." After this speech they agreed that this was right and should be done. [5]

The chiefs told their people about this and they said that they would do as Begochiddy had ordered. Kay-des-tizhi was to lead the men across the river and also take charge of the corn-grinding stones. So four big boats were made from a tree called Nash-konh and they named the boats Nash-konh after the tree. Kay-des-tizhi took all his goods and property and all of the male children and loaded them into one boat, and Begochiddy watched and saw that all the males crossed over the river. All went except a young Blue Fox man and a young Yellow Fox man, Mah-ih-doklizhi-sethkinh (Blue Fox Handsome Man) and Mah-ih-klitsoji-sethkinh (Yellow Fox Handsome Man). Both had flutes, and at night while the women were grinding corn they played their flutes to them. The flutes were made of small bamboo and when the women heard them, they laughed and had a merry time. Begochiddy soon found out that he had overlooked the two Foxes, and he made them go across the river to the rest of the males.

The men were strong and well-fed as they had plenty of corn and beans, and tobacco; and they made farms; and Kay-des-tizhi was their cook. The women also planted corn and beans, but the harvest was very poor; the corn was scanty and wormy; and their clothing was wearing out as they had no new skins to make new clothing. Estsan-natah, Head Woman, came up to Begochiddy and begged him to let them go back to the men as the women were very poor and hungry, and were tired of living alone. Begochiddy said: "Very well, all is forgiven; go back to your men, but I make for you this third law— 'the male shall rule and whatever your chiefs say, that must be done.'" They all agreed to this and then Begochiddy said: "If any other evil thing happens, I will make a flood to destroy you," and the women all said: "Very well, we will keep the home clean, cook the food, and care for the children." So the females were all taken across to the males, and they started to make new clothes of

26

cotton and deer skins of which the men had plenty. The men had plenty of food, meat, and corn, but they did not have any beads.

One day Estsa-assun and Asheen-assun went walking by the Water-Crossing-Place or whirlpool called Away-nah-olth, and there they saw a baby floating in the middle of the whirlpool. They went and told the gods about the baby, which had long black hair. Etsay-hashkeh, after hearing this from the women, said to himself: "I think I will go and see this baby," and he went towards the whirlpool from the east, then from the other three directions, south, west, and north, and each time he saw the baby floating. When he came from the fourth direction, he lifted the baby out of the water and hid him under his white robe, which was called Mah-ih-jilthli-lakai, and he kept the baby hidden inside of his robe for four days.

Four days after the baby had been stolen, a great noise began to sound in the east, south, west and north. And though Begochiddy knew what this meant, he told a crow to go to the east to see what was the matter, and the crow came back and said a storm was coming. To the south he sent a magpie, who saw a big blue storm coming. To the west he sent a humming bird, who saw a yellow storm coming. To the north he sent a dove, who found a white storm there. And the six gods went in all four directions gathering the plants, animals, and everything that had so far been created. They placed them in Lukatso, the big bamboo.

Estsan-natah, Head Woman, said to her son-in-law, Etsay-Hasleen: "I know many prayers and you know many songs to protect us." And she said to him also: "From now on, all the people who have been good and kind will go up to the fourth world, but all the bad people will go down to the first world, or Burning-Pitch-Place."

Meanwhile big storms were approaching from the four directions, and Begochiddy told Estsan-natah to sing her songs to protect the people. From this origin come the three first ceremonies. One ceremony is the story of the Ethkaynah-ashi; another the prayer and song; and another the song only. But no ceremony was held at the time of the creation. The songs and prayers used at that time are still used in the ceremonies. If people are bad and know this ceremony and ask for forgiveness, they need not go to the burning world. If a man kills another and repents and knows the ceremony he need not go down to the lower world, and the name of the ceremony is Chalth-yilth-nahgih-eh, or Wanderer-in-the-Dark. It can be held for sickness, when the sickness results from crime. The spirit of the Ethkaynah-ashi is the spirit of life and also is the spirit of the Wanderer-in-the-Dark.

There were two spirits who did not go up to the fourth world, one male and one female. The female was named Kith-nah-ha-klithy, which is the Spirit of Dusk which works with the Spirit of Darkness who is the male spirit, Kith-nah-kliz-hini. The female spirit lived in the house of red fire, Konth-lachee, with a door made of smooth wind, Niltche-dil-kohni. The male spirit lived in the House of Darkness, Chalth-yilth-hogahn, with a door named Nehochee-dothinlah.

Now the hot waters named Toh-bazdezkih and Toh-bazdeznah were rushing upon Lukatso (big reed) and all the creatures and plants hurried to get into it. But it would not start to grow, so they moved it to Tohe-egleen, where the waters meet, but it would not grow there, so they moved it again to Nahhodoh-othle, quicksand spring, where it began to grow at once. The turkey people did not get into the bamboo but clung outside to its joints, and, as the water rose, their tail feathers dipped into the white foam, which has made their tail feathers white on the ends to this day. As the water rose, they would climb up to the next joint until the water rose to it, and then they would climb up to another joint. The Lukatso kept growing until it could grow no more, and still it was not high enough to reach the next world, so Begochiddy made a white cloud above it and the people climbed up to it while the Spider Woman and the Spider Man wove a web around the edge of it to prevent the people from falling off.

Begochiddy saw that the chiefs and people were excited, so he called a Council to see what they could suggest about how to reach the upper world. The wolf chief had a white corn stalk in his hand and was dressed in the white tail feathers of the eagle. The lion chief had yellow corn in his hand and was dressed in the yellow tail feathers of the eagle. The lion and wolf knew that someone had done wrong to bring about such danger from the waters and asked their people who had sinned, and the people accused the chiefs because they said that they themselves had done nothing wrong. Begochiddy told the lion and the wolf that because they did not please the people they could not be chiefs any longer. And so the mocking bird and humming bird chiefs were the only ones left to govern, and they tried to find out who had done wrong but could not succeed. Begochiddy knew the sinner and also knew the people's thoughts.

Among those at the Council was the chief of the locusts who wore an arrow on his forehead made of an eagle tail. He asked Begochiddy why he had called the Council, and Begochiddy answered: "The people are afraid of the waters and do not know how to get into the upper world," and the Locust said: "I know how to reach there. Call the Ant People who are living at Nehochee."

So the Ant People were asked to try to dig a hole through to the upper world (this is called the Black Trail), but they could not succeed. And the yellow ants then tried, but they had to give it up (this is called the Yellow Trail). Meanwhile the Turkey People were making noises because their tails were still dipping in the water as they clung to the outside of the bamboo. Begochiddy asked the tiny black ants if they could dig through to the upper world (their road is called the Sparkling Trail), but they could not. So Begochiddy said to the Locust chief: "Sechai (Grandfather), please show us how to reach the next world." And the Locust put his arrow on his forehead and shot up into the next world. He had great powers.

Fourth World

The Locust came up through the crust and then through mud and water, for water covered the whole fourth world, and over it was flying a great white bird, Cheestehi-lakai. He had arrows with him and when he saw the Locust, he flew at him to kill him, but the Locust splashed water about, and the bird could not find him. The great bird asked the Locust: "Where did you came from, and who are you?" To show the Locust his power he took his arrow and swallowed it and then drew it out again, and asked the Locust if he could do anything like that, for if he could it would prove that he was great and powerful, and could live on the fourth world. The Locust had now come to the top of the water and was floating on it, resting with crossed legs. And he answered the great bird: "Yes, I can do that; watch me!" And he thrust his arrow through his heart and drew it out again, saying to the bird: "Can you do that? I have more power than you." So the bird was frightened and flew off to the east, and was not seen again.

From the south now came a big blue bird who tested the power of the Locust by thrusting his arrow twice down his throat; and the Locust conquered him by thrusting his arrow twice through his heart, and the blue bird flew back to the south.

A great yellow bird came from the west who swallowed his arrow three times, and the Locust thrust his arrow through his heart three times, and the yellow bird flew west again.

From the north came a white bird, and thrust his arrow down his throat four times, then the Locust thrust his arrow through his heart four times, and the bird flew north again. So the Locust won the contest of power with the great birds in this world.

Meanwhile the people still in the bamboo were very nervous because it was waving about in the air and they did not know what was happening to the Locust. When he came back by the hole to the lower world and began to speak to the people in the bamboo, his voice made a chee-chee sound because of the hole through which he had thrust his arrow. He told them that he had had a hard time getting up into the upper world, and he told them about the water, and of his trial of strength with the big birds, and he called the people his grandchildren.

Begochiddy asked all the chiefs and captains of the people: "Who will go up to the fourth world?" But no one would go, so Begochiddy went himself, and when he reached the upper world, he came out on a big pile of mud in the middle of the water.

To the east he saw a great white cloud, and he made a Rainbow Lightning which carried him to this cloud. And when he reached it, he found there Hashje-altye, the great god of the Yeh-bechai, and Hashje-altye was glad to see him and said: "How are you, my grandson? I own this world and have great power. The big birds tried to claim this world but I have conquered them and they are my servants." They were very happy together and then Begochiddy went back running on the water to the pile of mud at the center of the world.

Then he saw a blue cloud to the south with showers dropping from it, and he went there on the Rainbow and found Beganaskiddy, Bringer of Seeds, who welcomed Begochiddy and they were happy together. Beganaskiddy greeted Begochiddy as Hashje-altye had done and afterwards Begochiddy ran back on the water to the center of the world.

Then seeing a yellow cloud in the west, he went there on the Rainbow and found Hashje-hogahn, and they had the same intercourse as Begochiddy had had with the other gods, and then he went back to the center of the world running on the water.

To the north there was a white cloud, raining, and Begochiddy went there on the Rainbow, and found another Beganaskiddy. The same ceremony took place, and then he came back to the center of the world again.

Meanwhile Lukatso, the bamboo, was still swaying about, and the people inside of it were very much worried.

Begochiddy stood on the pile of mud at the world's center and saw Hashje-altye, the two Beganaskiddy, and Hashje-hoahn standing up to their breasts in the water at the east, south, west and north of the world. And Begochiddy waved his hand to each god in turn and they rose as he greeted them onto the surface of the water. then Hashje-altye took his cane and pushed the water back slowly to the east, and Beganaskiddy pushed harder to the south, Hashje-hogahn pushed harder still to the west, and Beganaskiddy at the north pushed hard so that the earth shook from the blow, and all the water ran off in different directions and made rivers. There was nothing where the water had lain but petrified wood and mud badlands, but there was water around all the earth and that was the ocean. Where the water had lain there were beasts who had been living in the water, but when Begochiddy blew on them they turned into strange shaped rocks, and as he continued to blow a crust formed on the mud. He looked to the east and saw figures away off, and he went towards them and found them to be gods, Yeh, with blue faces; Hashje-baka, male, and Hashje-ba-ahd, female; six males and six females. In the south there were the same gods, in the west the same, and in the north the same; and they were beautiful.

Begochiddy went back to the Lukatso, bamboo, and found the people much excited, and they were very glad to see Begochiddy, and when he came back to them they called him Sechai (Grandfather). He told them that he had met many people above, and that the world was good. They were very glad to hear that, and then Begochiddy sent Badger up to see the world. When he reached the hole, he tried to jump onto the crust but he broke through, and that is the reason why his paws are black to this day.

Begochiddy asked how the wet earth could be dried, and they sent up to the fourth world white thunder (Iknee-lakai) from the white mountain, also white cyclone (Niholtso-lakai) and white hail (N'dlohe-lakai), and black, blue and yellow cyclones. When the hail and thunder and cyclones hit the petri-fied wood and the mud columns which stuck up out of the mud, they were broken into pieces. Then the cyclones blew until they had dried the mud. And they sent live dust-devils, Nastol-disse, to trim up the rock pillars and make holes in them. After that five little whirlwinds were sent up, and they spread the tiny stones about smoothly.

Then the storms all went below to the third world from which they came, and the Lukatso began to grow again. And the people came up into this world led by the ants, with the turkey people coming last. Begochiddy pulled the bamboo up by the tassel on top and then threw the tassel back into the hole, which is why Lukatso, the bamboo, has no tassel now. This fourth world they called Hahjeenah.

The water from the third world came up into the hole after the people, and Begochiddy saw it and asked: "What is the reason that the water keeps com-ing up?" He blew and blew into the hole but could not stop it, and they were afraid it would overflow into this world. So the chief men held a council, and Etsay-Hasteen and all of them were very much worried and frightened, and each asked the other: "Who has done wrong and caused all this trouble?" Be-gochiddy said: "If none of you know who has done wrong, I think it may be Etsay-hashkeh, Coyote, who is the cause of it." And he went up to Etsay-hashkeh and opened his white robe and showed the baby he had stolen. It had yellow hands and looked very strange. Begochiddy took hold of the baby, but Etsay-hashkeh would not let it go, so Begochiddy dropped it, and Etsay-hashkeh threw the baby into the hole to the lower world, saying: "This is what has been the cause of the trouble." The baby fell on the forehead of a large water monster which was in the water at the bottom of the hole, and then the monster sank down in the water and took the baby down with it, and after that the water ceased to rise towards this world, and has always remained at that level.

There was nothing to make fire with in this new world, and the people wanted fire but did not know how to get it. The only person who had fire was Hashjeshjin, who kept away from the rest of the people. They saw smoke on the horizon far off, and Etsay-hashkeh, the Coyote, went over to see what it was. He found Hashjeshjin and Dontso (the white-headed fly) lying asleep, and all around them in four directions were river boulders burning like wood. And he stole some of the fire and ran back to the people and gave it to them.

Ceremony of Sweat-House Where Creation of This World Began

Begochiddy then called the people together and said: "Let us make plans as to how we shall live." But no one would plan at all and there were no ideas, so Begochiddy said: "Let us make a sweat-house for purification." "But what shall we build it of?" said the people. Begochiddy replied: "It is close to where Tchah, the Beaver, lives and we will borrow some material from him." Etsay-

Hasleen went and borrowed some sticks from the Beaver and brought back a lot as he had plenty.

The people then said: "There are no rocks here to build with," and Begochiddy said: "There are plenty, ask Deh-nozzi (the mountain sheep) for some." So Etsay-Hasleen went and got plenty of stone from the mountain sheep who said: "You are welcome to them."

The people asked: "What shall we have for fire?" Begochiddy said: "Go to Hasteen Dontso (the fly) and he will give you fire." He gave them fire gladly. And the people asked: "Where can we get water?" Begochiddy said: "Tabasteen-etahdeh, daughter of the Otter, will give you water." (They sing first of wood, then of stone on the wood, then of fire under the wood, and afterwards of bathing in the water.) For the roof house of the sweat-house they placed Rainbows, crossing from four directions to hold it up, and then the Robe of Darkness was placed over the Rainbows. Stones were brought and placed in the middle of the house. (They are now placed on one side of it.)

The people now asked: "What shall we have to cover the door?" Begochiddy replied: "Go ask Nasjah-hasteen, your grandfather, the Owl, and he will tell you." The Owl said: "Yes, I have white, blue, yellow and black colored robes and you may have as many as you wish, and I also have robes that flash." And the people chose a flashing robe and put it over the door, borrowing it from the Owl.

Then they all went into the sweat-house except Begochiddy, Hashjeshjin, Etsay-hashkeh and the women, for women were not allowed in the sweathouse. And they sang and Etsay-Hasteen led the singing. They sang of the fire, the stones, the wood, the water, and the sparkling robe, describing all of these things; and then they sang about the heat.

All the people who had loaned the things to make this sweathouse stood about outside; and the great Owl stood on the top of the roof, listening to the songs which described the things used in the sweat-house, and also thanked the givers for their help.

When the people came out of the sweat-house, Begochiddy told them to rub themselves with earth, which they did, thanking the earth as they did it. Then they went into the sweathouse again, and the Locust appeared and said: "I will sing for you." So they all went in together and the Locust sang to them. He sang about what he had done in helping the people to come up into this world, and about the contest with the great birds. Meanwhile the daughter of the Otter brought water in a wooden bowl and left it by the door outside, and when the people came out for the second time, they bathed in this water.

Then they went into the sweat-house again and began to plan to build some mountains on the earth. The first was Siss-nah-jini (Holy Mountain of the East), the next was Tsoll-tsilth (Mount Taylor), then Nahtah-has-eh (Mountain south of Zuñi), next Dogo-slee-ed (San Francisco Peaks), then Debeh-entsah (La Plata Mountains), next Tsilth-nah-ot-zithly (Huerfano

Mountain), next Johl-een (Pedernal Peak), next Tradadeen (a peak of the Jemez range).

Then they planned some rivers, Toh-bakahni, the male (San Juan) river, and Toh-ba-ad, the female (Rio Grande) water; then a lake, Hahjeenah, where the people came out of the bamboo (near Silverton, Colorado).

Then they planned some more mountains, Tsilth-lakai (White Mountains), Tsilth-kah-del-kah (Chuskai Mountains), Tsilth-il-entai (mountains near Chin Lee, Arizona), Tsilth-ti-del-tai (Sangre de Cristo range near Santa Fe, New Mexico), Tsilth-teen-del-tai (Jemez Mountain), Tsilth-beel-yah (Bill Williams Mountains south of San Francisco Peaks, Arizona). And then going westward towards California they planned these mountains, Tsilth-endes-kai, Tsilth-kis-lakai, Tsilth-dithklith, Tsilth-klitsoi, Tsilth-en-dokahnt, Tsilth-dogid-shegar, Tsilth-binneh-hasteen-tseel, Tsilth-neeteen-tseel, and Tsilth-ran-es-tseel (Bright Shining or Blue Mountain, on Santa Cruz Island, California).

Then they planned to create the Sun, Johonah-eh, and the Moon, Klayonah-eh, and many stars: the Morning Star, Sontso; the Evening Star, which is also Sontso; the North Star, Sontso-dohn-dohzeedi—The One That Does Not Move; and Sontso-deshyi, the Red Star Overhead. Also they planned the constellations: the Dipper, or Male Stars Going Around Like A Clock, Nohokos-bakahni; the little Dipper, or Female Stars Going Around, Nahokos-ba-ahdi; and the Pleiades or Seven Stars which is Dilgeheh. They planned also: Orion, Etsay-etsosi, the Thin Man; the Rabbit's Feet, Gah-atayjih; the Milky Way, Eekai-estahi; the Crown, Nashi-taythli; and Taurus, Bisolai or Two Stars Together; and the Great Snake of the North, Kleeshtso. They also planned Tah-zhuni, Smoky Star or Nebula; Dont-whutso, Two Stars Hooked Together; Sont-bidai, the Star With Horns; also Sont-eh-dekah, a Star Out of Sight in The East; and the Coyote Star, also in the east, called Mah-ih-besont. And all of these stars, mountains, the Sun, Moon and the rivers were planned while the people were in the sweat-house.

Then they began to plan the months. Each month had its own name and character and some of them had their own stars. The star for November was Hasteen-sikai (Old Man Bending Over); and this was called Niltche-tsosi, the Small Wind Month. The December star is Azay-tso (First Big Medicine), and it was called Niltche-tsoi, or Big, Cold-Wind Month. The January stars are Gah-atay-ih (Rabbit Tracks or Rattle), and this month was called Zus-entlis, or Thm, Icy Sheet. The February stars are Eekai-estahi (the Milky Way), and it was called Atsah-beyazh, or Young Eagle Month. March's name is Wooz-cheed (Noise Made by Eaglets), and it was called Iknee-tsosi or Little Thunder Month. April was called Tahn-chill (Small Growth), and the Canyon Wren belongs to that month, and its stars are Tuzhi-begay (Turkey Tracks). Another name for April is Sah-tah-debeh, meaning Mountain Sheep Have Lambs month, and a bird called Debeh-neh (Phoebe) also belongs to it. May was called Tahn-tso (Large Growth), and its star is Datsahni (Porcupine). June's name was Ayah-zush-chilly, meaning, Early-Greens-Are-Grown. Its star is Kleeshtso, or the Great Snake. July was called Ayah-zush-tso, meaning Large

33

Growth and Young Fawns month, and Wuzzy-gishi, the measuring worm, belongs to it. August's name was Binni-tahn-tsosi, meaning, Corn-Tassels-Have-Come, and the Anlthtahni, or Corn Bugs, belong to it. Its stars are all the small stars in the center of the sky. September was named Binni-tahn-tso, meaning When-Everything-is-Ripe, and Even-the-Mountains-are-Ripe. Its stars are Nahshalth-helee (the Ducks). October was called Gahnji, meaning Half-Winter-and-Half-Summer, and its star is Sontso-dohn-doh-zeedi, meaning North-Star-Stands-There.

These things they planned to make upon this world. And then they came out of the sweat-house and made another Hogahn of Rainbows called Hodayah which belonged to Kay-des-tizhi, the Man-Wrapped-in-a-Rainbow. And inside the Hogahn they spread many kinds of robes, and all six of the gods and all the Yeh gods and all the chiefs gathered in this Hogahn for a big Council.

And they sang the "Beginning of the World" song: "Nahteen, Song Odolith."

Nahteen Odolith

1st Verse

Nahastsan	odolith
Hodayah-dahnbith	odolith
Tas-ah	odolith
Sahanahray-bikay-hozhon	odolith
Tsilth-assun	odolith
Insontseel	odolith
Entklizhi-tas-eh	odolith
Kah-sah-oni	odolith
Tohe assun	odolith
Toh-ashtla-nascheen	odolith
Sahanahray-bikay-hozhon	odolith
Nahtahi-assun	odolith
Tradadeen-bith	odolith
Sahanahray-bikay-hozhon	odolith

2nd Verse

Elkaydahn-shehit-Taynizzen

3rd Verse

Hodayah-dahnven-ent-sissicasseh

4th Verse

Elkaydahn-bayaehl-gistsis

Note: This is in obsolete Navajo as told by Hasteen Klah and the following translation as he gave it to the interpreter.

34

Beginning of The World Song

It begins
"Creating the World
Creating the Mountain Gods
Creating mountain rain and creating beads and jewelry
Creating Sahanahray Bekayhozhon
Creating Mountain Man
Creating Little Rain on the Mountain
Creating jewelry and beads
Creating the holy spirit
Creating little rain spirit
Creating Sahanahray Bekayhozhon
Creating all mixed springs, lakes and ponds
Creating Sahanahray Bekayhozhon
Creating the Spirit of Creating
Creating the Spirit of Corn pollen
Creating Sahanahray Bekayhozhon."
The song is repeated three times, substituting for odolith (creating):
2nd Verse

> The beginning of the world, I knew about it before.

3rd Verse

> The beginning of the world, I am thinking about it.

4th Verse

> The beginning of the world, I am talking about it.

Repeating the rest of the song as in the first verse.

The spirits of all the things about to be created were also in the Hogahn with the gods and the chiefs. All the corn and all the seeds were brought by the Yeh gods at Begochiddy's request. Hashjeshjin brought all the stars, the Sun, the Moon, and all the Light, and the other people brought the rest of the things that were to be on this world. They were all in the Hogahn.

They decided to place the mountain Siss-nah-jini in the east. And they made a pile of dirt to represent it in the Hogahn. And they made the spirit for this mountain. And then all the mountains that have been named before in this story were placed in their proper positions in the Hogahn. They put the Sun in the east and the Moon in the west; and in the middle, they placed the Chuskai Mountains and Black Mountain, which is near Chin Lee, and also the Jemez Mountains. And they made a song about the creating of the mountains. And they made spirits like men and put them into all these mountains and into the Sun and the Moon.

Then they sang the song of the Holy Spirit of Darkness:

Hozhon-la-hozhon-la

Hozhon-la hozhon-la
Sahanahray-hozhoni-
  bikaygi-klizhin-entslee
Hozhon-la hozhon-la
Hozhon-la hozhon-la

which means: "The world is beautiful and we are going to put the spirit into it." While they were creating the spirits, they always sang.

Hashjeshjin and Choostaigi, who are the black gods and are brothers, now put their own spirits into the stars and the mountains, and these spirits were in human form in the likenesses of Hashjeshjin and Choostaigi. Then Begochiddy told the Council that all of the songs which had been sung since the making of the first world should be remembered by men forever; and that also they must remember all the names of the mountains. And all the other gods repeated what he had said. Etsay-Hasteen, the first male, and Estsa-assun, the first female, who have the spirit of sickness and give it to men if they do wrong, said to the people: "If you do not remember these things and reverence them, we will bring sickness upon you." And all the gods said the same. And the Yeh gods were appointed to watch over the people, and they gave flint to them so that they could get fire.

Begochiddy said: "We must hurry and create the Spirit-of-the-Earth, Na-hastsan-be-esteen, which is the Spirit that makes things grow." So they created this Spirit, who was painted with a yellow stripe across her mouth, a blue stripe across her nose, and on her eyes a black stripe and on her forehead a white stripe, and she had blue horns with black tips. The Spirit had eagle feathers on her head, and on the feathers were different kinds of birds, and in her hand she had a pollen basket, and she was wrapped in a blanket made of everything that grows on the earth.

Then they created the Spirit of the Sky, Yaah-dithklithy-be-esteen, the Rain and Cloud Spirit, who was dressed like the Earth Spirit except that he had black horns with blue at the ends. He had a head-dress of clouds and on the clouds were all kinds of rain and fog. And in his hand he carried a water jug, and he was wrapped in a black cloud robe. He controls the rain.

The earth and Sky Spirits are connected with corn pollen. Their hands and feet are clasped together, and the mouth of one of these Spirits is connected with the other. And also they have a black wind and a blue wind which work together and this is called Tradadeen-yeh-kaneh-de-azh. (There is a prayer about this which is part of the ceremony). Sahanahray and Bikay-hozhon are the Holy Spirits to the Earth and to the Sky.

They decided that the spirit of Siss-nah-jini, the Holy Mountain of the East, should be dressed in white shell beads, but the spirit of Tsoll-Tsilth (Mount Taylor) became jealous because he wanted to wear white shell, and they argued with him four times about it. Finally it was decided that Siss-nah-jini's spirit should be dressed in white shell with a big white shell for a head-dress.

And they gave him the white corn to carry. And his blanket was made of morning light. And they put a small white shell in his mouth.

Tsoll-tsilth's spirit was dressed in turquoise in the same way as Siss-nah-jini's, but his blanket was turquoise, and they gave him blue-birds, and they put turquoise in his mouth.

The spirit of Dogo-slee-ed (San Francisco Mountain) was dressed in abalone shell. They gave him yellow corn to carry, and his blanket was made of yellow sunset light, and in his mouth was put a small abalone shell.

The spirit of Debeh-entsah (La Plata Mountains) was dressed in jet. His blanket was a robe of night blackness, and he was given all the game, deer, sheep, antelope. And in his mouth was put jet.

The spirit of Tsilth-nah-ot-zithly (Huerfano Mountain) was dressed in all kinds of colored clothing, and they gave him a robe of agate and put in his mouth white crystals.

The spirit of Johl-een (Pedernal Mountain) was dressed in all kinds of jewelry, and his blanket was made of Rainbows, and they put corn pollen in his mouth.

There are two mountains which are built like men, the Chuskai Mountains and the Black Mountains. Niltsa-tseel, the Rainy Mountains (Chuskai range) was dressed in Natseen-nahi. His head is Beautiful Mountain. He has a turquoise rattle. His hand is a mountain near Lukachukai; his feet are two peaks west of Tohatchi; and the red patch of earth at Toadalena is his heart. The spirit of Tsilth-klizhin or Black Mountain, which is near Chin Lee, is dressed the same as the Chuskai Mountains, in Natseen-nahi. His feet are near Indian Wells; his tail is close to Ganado; the trail to Oraibi is his middle, and in the center of Black Mountain is a hollow space where his ribs are. His heart is in the Black Mountains and his head is north near the San Juan River. His hands are the cliffs northwest of his head, near Marsh Pass, and he had a big ear of corn in his hand, Tsa-kahn.

The mountains that they had built in the first world were now remade in this fourth world, and the Jemez and Sangre de Cristo Mountains were both dressed in turquoise. Santa Fe Mountain is called Tradadeen-tsilth (Corn Pollen Mountain), and Jemez Mountain is called Anlthtahni-tsilth (Corn Bug Mountain).

The Coyote now said: "Give me some dirt out of which you are making mountains!" But they refused, saying: "You are not clever enough to make mountains." He said: "Yes, I am clever enough." He asked this four times, and finally the gods gave him some of the earth which was left after making so many kinds of mountains, and the Coyote took it and made a peak in the south and decorated it with aloe. He said: "This will be called my mountain." It took the shape of his paws and it has that shape now, and is called Pagosa Peak.

Then they made the Sun of fire with a rainbow around it, and they put the Turquoise Man into the Sun as its spirit. (The Sun should be represented with woodpecker feathers around it and with horns.) The Moon was made of ice with a rainbow around it, and the spirit of the Moon was the White-Shell-Man. (The Moon should be represented with horns also.)

Then they made a black wind, and they put the spirit of the Abalone Man into it. This is the east wind. They then made a yellow wind and put the spirit of the Red Shell Man into it. The winds also have horns, and wear twisted wind robes around them. Then they made the Fall and Winter and put them in the north and west; and they made the Spring and Summer, and placed them in the south and east; each to be six months long. The Coyote claimed one month which was October, and Begochiddy made a prayer stick of Lukatso (bamboo), half yellow and half white, representing summer and winter, and gave it to him in answer to his claim. October is the mixed-up or changing month and is so known to all the Indians.

Then all the spirits which had been made went into the places where they belonged, and they raised the Sun and Moon and Stars and Winds and placed them in their proper places. They were all spirits. Hashjeshjin placed the North Star and said that everything was complete and that he was glad. Begochiddy said to Etsay-Hasteen: "Why do you not place some stars?" So Etsay-Hasteen made the Big Dipper and placed it, and dressed it in feathers, and gave it horns. And Estsa-assun also took stars and placed the Little Dipper. And Etsay-Hasteen also placed the Seven Stars. (Hashjeshjin claimed that the Seven Stars were on his foot, and on his knees and hips and back and shoulders, and on the side of his face.) Estsa-assun picked up another star, Etsay-etsosi, and placed it at the south. She also picked up another star, Etsay-etso, and placed it. And she placed the Milky Way and the Crown and the Porcupine Star, and the Southern Cross. Etsay-Hasteen arranged the Rabbit's Track and placed the Porcupine Star and the Horned Star and several others. They took turns in placing the stars. Then Etsay-Hashkeh, the Coyote, said: "Let me try," and he asked for two stars. So they gave him two, but he could not find a good place in which to place them, and had to put them close together, and called them the Fighting Stars. Then he asked them for another star and he placed it at the south near the horizon (Antares), and called it the Coyote Star. It goes to sleep after the Sun sets. He was still greedy and asked for more but was refused, so he filled both paws full of stars and threw them into the sky which made the tiny stars which cover it all over. Hashjeshjin's is the Cornet Star with a tail.

Then they placed twelve big white cyclones (Niholtso) in the east under the edge of the world, and twelve blue cyclones (Niholtso-doklizh), under the edge of the world at the south, and twelve yellow cyclones (Niholtzo-klitsoi) in the west under the edge of the world, and twelve black cyclones under the north. And these forty-eight cyclones are what hold the world up. They also sent all kinds of winds up to the Sky to hold up the sky and stars. The Indians have a wind prayer, Eyah-nos-zhini, which is to help these winds hold up the world. Begochiddy told them now to chew up the roots and herbs and then blow this medicine in different directions.

Then Begochiddy took the Ethkaynah-ashi and motioned toward all creation and it came to life. And the Sun started to rise in the east, and the Sun Spirit's heart started to beat. The Sun and the Moon moved quickly, and the Mountains and Stars slowly, and the eyes of the people in Council were paralyzed at seeing this movement. And everyone was petrified and called out: "What is the matter with our eyes, they won't move?"

Etsay-hashkeh, the Coyote, and Hashjeshjin knew why this happened, and Etsay-hashkeh jumped up and said: "I will explain it to you. The son-in-law and mother-in-law must not look at each other. It is like the stars; the constellation Etsa-tzo is the mother-in-law, and the constellation Dilgeheh is the son-in-law; and these stars must not meet. For the same reason mother-in-law and son-in-law must not see each other, and if they do their eyes will become blind." When they had understood this, their eyes ceased to be paralyzed.

They named the Earth Spirit, Nahastsan-be-esteen, and the Sun, Johonaheh and the Sky Spirit Yaah-dith-klithy-be-esteen, and the Moon, Klayonah-eh, and the two mountains, Siss-nah-jini and Tsoll-tsilth. And while they were being named, the Coyote said: "Tsoll-tsilth is my name and I want it," but they said: "No, you cannot have it, your name is Mah-ih (thief)." He said: "I am not a thief," and he was very angry and sent his spirit to trouble Tsolltsilth (Mount Taylor) which began to slide down, so that the gods had to put a lot of small peaks of Malpais (badlands) around the mountain to stop it from slipping, and the little peaks succeeded in holding it, and they are still doing so. They asked Tsoll-tsilth if he was all right now, and the Mountain said that he was quite comfortable. He cut the hair off from one side of his head so that there are trees on one side only today. Then the Council named all the mountains in their order and they all went where they are today.

First Death and First Movement of Creation

Everything was in its place, but the Earth, Sky, Sun, and Moon did not move and the Coyote said the reason was that a person was going to die. (Begochiddy told this to the Coyote and the Coyote told the people.) Then the first person died, who was called Etsay-dassalini, and at once the Earth and the Sun and Moon began to move again and the Sun said: "I am glad when a person dies as that is what keeps me moving, and I am glad to keep moving."

Begochiddy planted everything that grew, and made everything that breathed, and took the Ethkaynah-ashi and motioned toward all creatures and plants and they came to life. He appointed the seasons for everything that grew and they answered: "We will do as we are told." And all creation started and the ants began building houses. The first time that the Sun crossed the sky, it was too near the Earth and it was too hot. The second time it still was too hot. The third time it was still too hot, but the fourth time it was exactly in the right place and it has stayed there ever since.

Etsay-Hasteen asked: "Where has the life gone from the man who died?" No one knew, so he kept on asking all the people until he came to Begochid-dy, who answered him: "I will hunt for it." So he hunted for a long time but could not find the life that had gone until he looked down into the Third World, and there he saw the man who had died brushing his hair, his face painted red. And Begochiddy came to the people and said: "I have seen the man who died down below in the Third World. I saw him with the shadow of the Ethkay-nah-ashi. You must live holy lives, for the people who do wrong go down to the Burning-Pitch-Place, where there is an enormous monster who devours people." The people who go down there are called Chindi or Devils.

Begochiddy then said to the people: "I am going to heaven now, but I will come back in two days. Watch me go up." And they all watched him as he went straight up into the air.

At this time Has-estrageh-hasleen died, and he was the second man to die. When Begochiddy came back in two days, he said it was a very beautiful place up there in heaven, and that he had seen Has-estrageh-hasleen in a very beautiful place, sitting surrounded by flowers and smelling of them, and Begochiddy said: "All who believe in my word will go up to heaven, but all who do wrong or think wrong will go down to where the pitch is burning."

While Begochiddy was in heaven, he made a man called Begothkai, whom he called his son, and brought back with him to earth. He was a short man, white in flesh, with black eyes and black hair and with a white face.

Begothkai spoke to the people and told them to move to Nahtee-tseel (north of Durango, Colorado) where there are four mountains in a line, and after they had done as he told them then they could live wherever they liked, Then Begochiddy and his son went back to heaven and Day and Night came to the earth as they come today. Begothkai never has come down again from heaven.

When the people first emerged from the lower world, they had seen a Yeh over on Mount Taylor, Tson-tsilth, but he was small and they were not afraid. Now they saw him again, and he had grown very large and had a very big nose, small eyes, and black whiskers on his chin. They realized that he had turned into a giant. When they first saw him, they thought he was a Yeh but now they knew that he was a Yehtso or Big Giant. (The reason that the giant lived on Tsoll-tsilth was because Tsoll-tsilth was a badly behaved mountain which had argued about its name and had asked to dress in white shell beads). The Sun claimed the giant and called him his son, although he really was not related to him, and the Sun took the giant to his home and dressed him with stone shoes and clothing of Bezh or obsidian to protect him from his enemies. And he gave him the Lightning Arrow (Iknee-kah) as a weapon for his right hand, and a stone knife for his left hand. When he had dressed him, the Sun took the Yehtso on a streak of lightning and went to Tsoll-tsilth. The giant had a hot spring, Toh-sit-toh, from which he drank, and though the people lived far from this place, when the giant would call "singo," the people were forced to come to him, and then he would eat them. Then the people saw another kind of monster called Dah-il-kadeh who lived at Black Lake (near Pueblo Bonito, New Mexico). This monster had twelve antelopes guarding him, and when the antelopes saw any person within reach they told Dah-il-kadeh and he ran out and grabbed them and then ran backward on his own track to his den. Dah-il-kadeh looks like a gopher but is enormous. He hunted in all four directions, and the people were very much afraid of him as he was very fierce. They never went near him, but he could often catch them as he could run very fast.

There was an enormous bird, Tseh-nah-hahleh, who lived at Ship Rock, Tseh-ed-ah, who had a very long beak, very large eyes, and his claws were very long and sharp, and he ate people. He had two little ones in his nest whom he had to feed.

There also was a man made of stone who lay stretched out on a hill beside the river just west of the Aztec Ruins. When anyone walked past he would kick them into the San Juan River, and when they were drowned, he would feed them to his two children. He was called Tseh-ed-ah-eh-delklithy, which means Kicking Rock. His children lived in the river and ate the drowned people.

Also on the top of the Jemez Mountains there was a great hollow place called Nehochee-otso, and there lived a great striped rock which could roll very quickly in any direction, and killed people by rolling on them. It was called Tseh-nagi, Rolling Rock.

Then on the east side of Blue Water, New Mexico, there was a red mountain where a lot of black insects lived who killed people by looking at them. They stared at a person until he was paralyzed, and then they ate him. They were called Benan-yah-runi, or Staring-Eyes-That-Kill.

Where the La Plata River meets the San Juan River lived an immense centipede who was very fierce and treacherous, and could run very fast. He had many young ones who helped to eat the people. He was called Sil-dil-hushy-tso, the One-Who-Bites.

There was also a Crushing Rock, or Rocks-That-Come-Together, just west of Taos Mountain. This was called Tseh-ah-kin-dithly.

Dohgah-tyelth, west of the Chama River, was the place of Luka-ih-digishi, the Cutting Reeds. Here many trails led into the reeds, and when any one passed through them, the reeds moved and cut the person into little pieces and ate him. If no one was among the reeds they remained perfectly quiet.

Another monster was called Tseh-ko, a narrow black canyon north of Taos. If a person tried to step across it, it widened and they fell in and were killed.

Up in the Canjilon Mountains there was a place called Siss-pai. There were big cactuses called Hoosh-esh-entsiah-etso, and many trails led among them. When people walked through the trails the cactus would close and catch them. They had heads like human beings, and when a person was caught on the spines of the cactus, he stayed there until he dried up.

On the Mancos River lived the Tushgizhi-ent-dil-kizhi, Rock Swallows. They were very bad birds. They would rush out at people, striking them and clawing them at once.

At Tsilth-entsah, there lived four bears, Shush-nah-kahi (Bears-That-Trail). These monsters were killing many people, who were in despair, and did not know how to fight them.

The Saving of Created Beings

At Tsilth-nah-ot-zilthy, the small Huerfano Mountain, were living Etsay-Hasteen, Estsa-assun, and Etsay-hashkeh (First Man, First Woman and Coyote). They were not in danger from the monsters because they went about in a cloud. By this time the people were being killed off so fast that only a few were left. And Begochiddy came down from heaven and when he saw how the people were suffering, he took pity on them and said he would preserve them. He told them he would put a pair of every living creature into a large flute made of big bamboo which belonged to Etsay-Hasteen. And all the creatures said: "Very well, we are willing to go." And they got into the flute and it flew off with them. They flew to Siss-nah-jini and from there they flew four times around all the mountains, and then they flew to a big peak called Tsilth-lapai-ah, north of San Francisco Peak. In this peak there was a large cave. The people got out of the flute and went into the cave and lived there, all except Etsay-hashkeh, Etsay-Hasteen, Estsa-assun and Asheen-assun, who flew away in the flute back to Huerfano Peak. Every day they flew about invisibly and every night they went back to Huerfano. They saw a lot of Yehtso-lapai, or grey monsters, walking about. These were large-eyed, fish-eyed, foolish and crazy people, and very bad. They carried baskets on their backs and were very poor and wore grass clothing.

Creation of Estsan-Ah-Tlehay

Begochiddy asked the four gods in the flute if they were lonely. And they said that they were very lonely now that all the people who had been created were hidden in the cave because of the monsters. So Begochiddy told the First Woman, Estsa-assun: "I will come back in four days and see what can be done," And after four days he came back and said: "This night I will show you."

Then a great Star appeared over Johl-een (Pedernal Mountain). And the star, which was Hashjeshjin (the Fire God), sent a Light-ray down to the mountain. Begochiddy came again and asked what they had seen, and they told him that they had seen a bright light on Johl-een. And while they were talking, Hashje-altye (the Talking God) came dressed in a rainbow and a shiny feather head-dress. And he spoke four times to them. The people told him to go and see why there was light on the mountain and he said: "Very well, I will go and find out about it."

When Hashje-altye came to Johl-een, he saw the Light-ray connecting the mountain and the sky, and looking like an immense shining cloud or rainbow. Hashje-altye went towards the mountain and heard the Bluebird, Dohleh, singing. And he came to the mountain from the west side, and he heard all sorts of birds singing. And when he came from the north he heard the pollen or corn bird, Ahn-enteni. Then he went back from the north, to the west, then to the south, then to the east side and stood there. And then he went up to the mountain and there he found a very fine newly-born baby girl, with flowers surrounding her. Hashje-altye was very glad to see this, and went back to tell Begochiddy and the others what he had found. Begochiddy knew all about the baby, as he had seen it, and he said to the people: "It is the child of the Earth Spirit and the Sky Spirit."

Then the gods went and found the baby, bringing gifts with them. Estsa-assun brought a white shell basket, Etsay-Hasteen a fine water bowl; Asheen-assun (Salt Woman) brought soap root. They were going to wash the baby then, but before doing so they asked all the mountains and peaks if they could take care of it and wash it, but the mountains and peaks could not agree as to which should undertake the care of the child and so all refused. Begochiddy came down and told the gods to take the baby to Lukasahkah-tso (Alamo) and wash the baby there at that spring, and then to take her back to Tsilth-nah-ot-zilthy (Huerfano Peak) and there to make a hogahn out of mirage to be called Hadahonigay-be-hogahn.

They did all that Begochiddy commanded, and loved the baby very much, and guarded it closely. And the mountains also loved the baby.

They made a cradle of the straight lightning for it, and placed a rainbow at the foot of the cradle, and they decorated the cradle with a rainbow, and the bow over the top of the cradle was made of a rainbow. The Salt Woman was sent to get something soft for the baby to lie on, and she shredded bark for it, and this same bark today is used for babies' cradles. The cradle was called Away-estsa.

The robe in which the baby was wrapped was made of a beautifully patterned cloud, and over it they wrapped the baby in another white cloud robe, and used a very fine white rock powder to rub in all the baby's creases. The Salt Woman called the baby her sister. They then motioned to the baby with the Ethkaynah-ashi and gave it life, and the baby started to cry.

Hashje-altye spoke to the others and said: "How can we feed the baby?" And they tried to feed it on pollen, but it did not agree with the baby, so Hashje-altye said: "It would be better to give the baby to Hashje-ba-ahd (the female Yeh), and she would know how to bring it up and take care of it." The gods who had the baby would not agree to this. They loved the baby so much they would not give it up to any one and they said they could feed the baby on the pollen of the white shell. So Hashje-altye agreed that they should take care of it. Hashje-hogahn (the House God) also asked for the baby, as he had daughters who would take care of it and feed it from the pollen of the afterglow of the sunset, but the gods refused to let him have the child. They fed the baby with the white inside bark of the cedar tree mixed with pollen, but the baby did not like it and spat it out. Then they fed her with the white shell pollen and the flower pollen, and she liked this and flourished.

When she was two years old, she was able to walk about and one of the Yehtso-lapai, a Grey Monster, tried to steal her, but fortunately Etsay-Hasteen saw the Yehtso climbing up the mountain looking for the baby. The Yehtso could not see the baby but he found her tracks, and Etsay-Hasteen said to the monster: "There is no baby here. I made these tracks that you have found with my hands." Four times Etsay-Hasteen drove the Yehtso-lapai away.

Asheen-assun, the Salt Woman, was the nurse of the baby and guarded her. And once upon a time a good many of the Yehtso-lapai managed to see the Salt Woman with the baby and they tried to climb up the mountain to reach them but found it too difficult. After this happened, Etsay-Hasteen planted a great many little cactus plants around the mountain so that when the Yehtso-lapai attempted to climb over them they cried out with pain and did not dare to cross the cactus in order to steal the baby.

When she was about six years old and had lost her baby teeth, they made her another set of teeth of white shell, and told her when she rose in the morning to throw her old teeth toward the east.

Maiden Ceremony for Estsan-Ah-Tlehay

When she was sixteen years old, they had the Maiden Ceremony for her called Hozhonigi, or Making-the-Path-of-Life-Beautiful. They dressed her in white shell shoes, fine deer-skin robes and the finest sort of shell and turquoise ornaments. Her hair was parted in the middle and hung down tied at the back half way to the ends. They invited Kay-des-tizhi, the Man-Wrapped-in-a-Rainbow, and he came and brought many different shell dishes and food, and also he brought her a baby lamb; and all the gods came; also the Yeh.

The ceremony began with a race between the Salt Woman and the girl before sunrise every morning for four days. On the night of the fourth day, they sang the Creation Song, which has twenty-four verses. Etsay-Hasteen sang it first and the others after him, and they sang until daybreak. Etsay-Hasteen also had a song he sang while the girl and woman raced before sunrise, which is called Sheyash-estsa-sohni, or Young-Woman's-Race. They told the Earth Spirit about this ceremony and he sent the white and red paint with which they painted her cheeks red, and they painted two small white stripes on each cheek. They sang of painting the maiden, Zhan-sheya-yanez-nuchee. Begochiddy told the people that he wanted them to paint their faces in the same way. Those who begin the painting of their faces at the top and paint down to the chin signify that they are asking for rain; those who paint from the chin up to the forehead are asking for anything that grows. So they painted their faces, and brought many robes and piled them in a heap on top of one another at the door of the Mirage Hogahn where the girl lived.

Then she lay face down flat on this pile of robes and her hair covered her whole body. Estsa-assun stroked her hair and face and body to make her fine and strong. After that they gave her the lamb which Kay-des-tizhi had brought her, and she held it to her breast as she lay on the pile of blankets.

Begochiddy asked the people what name they were going to give this girl but they all stood silent. And while they watched her she grew older and older until she was a bent old woman, and even as they watched her, she grew a little younger again, and before their eyes she changed four times from youth to age, but at the fourth change she remained about twenty years old, and she was very beautiful. Begochiddy named her White Shell Woman, Yolthkai-estsan, and the rest of the people called her by that name. From this time onward, she would always be able to grow old or young as she desired and so she was called also Estsan-ah-tlehay, or Changing Woman.

Then she rose from the pile of robes and gave the lamb back to Kay-des-tizhi, the Man-wrapped-in-a-Rainbow. And the people turned their backs to her, and she went to each one in turn and took their heads in her hands and lifted them a little to thank them for their gifts. Begochiddy gave her a big basket full of flowers and she gave the flowers to the people who put them in their hair, and all went away again very happy and thankful. In the basket of flowers which she had passed around, there were a lot of poison weeds named Johnjilway, Toh-o-whetso, Asgai-binee, Ajah-tohee, but no one received them; they only received the good flowers and the poison weeds were taken back into the hogahn.

Mating of The Sun and Estsan-Ah-Tlehay

One day the maiden was gathering wood, and suddenly felt some one touch the bundle of wood which she carried. She was terrified, dropped her wood, and ran home. When she got there, Estsa-assun asked her what was the matter and reassured her, and told her to go back again and get some more wood. She was twenty-two years old now, and though at first she did not know who had touched her, she found out that it was the Sun Spirit who had fallen in love with her.

After this, during six months, she and the Sun Spirit did not see each other and were separated; and this separation was called Toh-n'del-kous.

Birth of Nayenezgani and Tohbachischin

About six months after the separation of the maiden and the Sun, twins were born to her called Nayenezgani, who was the elder, and Tohbachischin, and they had the same sort of cradle as was made for their mother. They did not eat anything for four days after they were born. They gave them cedar bark at first to eat but it did not agree with them, and after four days their mother began to feed them and they flourished. At two years old, they could walk and play around the hogahn. It is said that at Huerfano Peak (Tsilth-nah-ot-zilthy) where they lived, the tracks of the boys are still to be seen. Hashje-altye and Begochiddy came often to see the boys, as they loved them very much, and at four years old they were both quite big and strong. When they were seven years old, they both lost their teeth and their mother put white shell teeth in the place of the ones they had lost. They threw away their old teeth towards the east and it is said that all teeth that are thus thrown away are given to the Badger, Tabasteen.

When they were sixteen years old, they were quite grown up, and they looked so much alike no one could tell them apart. They wanted very much to find out who their father was. They asked this four times before the Sun had risen, but their mother was ashamed to tell them. But when the Sun had come up about half way, she pointed to it and said: "That is your father."

Etsay-Hasteen made the twins bows and arrows, and they went about hunting and enjoying themselves. Once in their wanderings they came close to the edge of the mountain and they saw a Yehtso, a Gray Monster, coming up, and they shot at him with their bows and arrows and he was so frightened that he ran away.

One day when they were out hunting, Begochiddy met them and sitting down between them said: "The Sun is your father and you must go and visit him." To help them, and to tell them what would happen in the future, and to show them the way, he gave them wind spirits, Niltche-beyazh. And he gave Nayenezgani the elder, the rainbow, Natseelit, to carry him wherever he wanted to go. And he gave Tohbachischin a ray of light, Shah-bekloth. He told the boys that when they came to their father's house they would be shown all sorts of clothing and other things, but that they must choose only the flint armor, Bezh; the lightning arrows, Iknee-kah; and the stone knife, also the big cyclones and the big hail, and the kehtahn or magic cigarette named Kehtahn-de-konth; and he repeated: "You must be sure to ask for that." (Their mother, Estsan-ah-tlehay, did not know that they were starting on this journey.)

Beginning of Their Journey to The Sun

Then Nayenezgani stood on the rainbow and Tohbachischin stood on the ray of light and Begochiddy breathed on the rainbow and the ray of light and started them on their way. After flying some distance through the air, they walked on the earth again for some distance, but they came to a great sand-dune called Sals-ah which they could not cross on foot. So they mounted their rainbow and ray of light and were carried over that obstacle. They walked again for some distance but had to mount into the air on their magic rainbow and ray to cross a very big canyon. Then they walked again until they came to a very big cactus when again they used their magic arrows. And again they walked until they were stopped by many reeds and they crossed them in the same magic way.

Again they walked on and came to a big river. At the edge of the river they found a lot of water-bugs who asked the twins where they were going, and the boys said that they were going to cross the river, and the bugs said: "We will help you." And they bunched themselves together and took the boys on their backs and carried them over. After they had crossed the river they met a meadow-lark who asked them: "Where are you going, my grandsons? Your father is very angry, so I will give you a song to help you when you meet him." So the meadow-lark sang a song to them and they went on their way.

Suddenly a woman jumped out of the ground before them who had a spider web in her hand, and she was the Spider Woman. She invited the boys to come into her home but the boys thought the doorway was too small and that they could not get in. The Spider Woman knew what they were thinking so she blew four times at the doorway and each time that she blew the doorway grew larger until finally it was large enough for the boys to enter. The Spider Woman said to them: "Your father is not kind, so I will teach you a song to help you, and also give you an eagle's pin-feather which will protect you."

The boys went on their way until they met four old women who asked them: "Where are you coming from?" The boys pointed to their home and the old woman said to the boys: "Your father is not kind, so we will give you a song to help you." These were the first old people in the world and if they had not met the boys, no one would ever grow old now. The twins went on and met an older woman who would not speak to them and later they met a still older woman. Then the twins came to the Daybreak, and they went on under it until they came to the After-glow-of-Sunset and went on under it, then under the Dusk, then under the Darkness until they came to a place where many children were playing, and this place was called Yeh-kai-beyazhi, and they crossed this place on their rainbow and light ray. And they then went up into the Black Sky and came to the Turquoise House, Hogahn-doklizh, which is always in darkness.

On the wall outside near the door of the house was a large hook on which the Sun was hung, while the Spirit of the Sun lived inside the house. In the Turquoise House were four rooms, one east, one south, one west, and one north, and there were many little Suns there, and all sorts of bright lights to make it light. Two Thunder-birds, Iknee, were guarding the door, but the boys entered the house without being molested by the guards although they saw the twins. The second guard over the house was the Water Monster, Te-oltsodi, and the third guard was the big snake, Kleeshtso. The fourth guard was the mountain lion, Nashtui-l'tso, and the boys passed all of them.

Test of The Twins by The Sun

Inside on the east side of the house there was a black cloud rolled up, on the south side a blue cloud, on the west a yellow cloud, and on the north a white cloud. The twins met the Moon Spirit there, though the Moon itself was not present as it was wandering about. And the Spirit asked them: "What are you doing here, my boys? Your father is a fierce man and I will try to protect you." So the Spirit wrapped the two boys in the white cloud to hide them.

After they were hidden in the white cloud, the Sun Spirit came in and asked the Moon Spirit: "Who was speaking?" and the Moon Spirit answered: "No one except myself." The Sun Spirit did not believe this and went to the black cloud and unrolled it but found nothing there, and he unrolled the south cloud and the west cloud, and finally in the north cloud he round the boys. He seized them by the hair of their heads and threw them against some great spikes of obsidian which were turned edge-wise like knives set in the floor at the east side of the hogahn. He said: "I hope these boys are my sons" (for if they were really his sons they would not be hurt by anything). They were not harmed by the knives; and then the Sun Spirit threw them onto the knives on the south, west and north, and they were still unharmed.

The Sun Spirit called the Moon Spirit and said: "Uncle, heat the sweat-house." So the Moon Spirit heated the sweat-house, and on one side he dug a hole large enough to contain the two boys and covered it with a little Moon. He brought the boys over to the sweat-house and showed them the hole where they could hide, and they hid themselves in it. Then the Sun Spirit came to the house bringing a jug of water and poured it on a bar of obsidian which had been heated red hot; and it filled the house with much steam, and he asked the boys: "Are you too warm in there?" and the boys answered: "No." He asked this of the boys four times and they answered each time: "No, we are all right," so the Sun Spirit went back to his hogahn and the boys came out of the sweat-house.

Each night while they were at the Sun's house they slept on the roof, and they had a robe of white clouds to cover them and the Sun Spirit gave them another robe also, but they were very cold there and would have frozen except that the Otter Woman came and gave them her fur robe to spread over them. It hailed and stormed all night, and the Sun thought that they would be frozen, but thanks to the fur robe which the Otter Woman gave them they were warm.

When the Sun went into his home again, he filled a turquoise pipe, a white shell pipe, an abalone pipe, and a jet pipe with poison smoke. On their way back to the Sun's house from the sweat-house, the twins met a caterpillar who gave them some medicine weeds to eat so that they could not be killed if they smoked the poison pipes of the Sun. Back in the Sun's house again the boys were given a blue pipe to smoke, and the Sun lighted it with a little Sun. They smoked all of the pipes easily.

Finding that he could not kill them with the poison smoke, the Sun Spirit caught the boys by the hair and threw them into a big black jar on the east side of the room. He then hung a huge stone by a stream of water to the roof over the jar and let the stone fall to crush the twins; but when he looked into the jar, he saw the boys in it unharmed. He tried this four times, and even made the great stone drop more heavily but he could not hurt the twins.

Then he took the boys into his arms, holding one on either side of him, for he knew now that they were really his sons, because they had not been harmed by his tests.

The Sun Spirit had four children by a spirit woman named Yoodi-yenai, who had been in the Fourth World. Her eldest daughter was called Turquoise Girl, Doklizhe-etahdeh, and the younger was called White Shell Girl, Yolthkai-etahdeh. The older boy was called Abalone Boy, Dichithli-eshki, and the younger boy was called Jet Boy, Baszhini-eshki. The Sun Spirit said to his daughters: "Bring some water to your brothers," and the Turquoise Girl brought a blue basket and a jug of water, and the White Shell Girl brought a white basket and a jug of water, and also they brought soap-root, and the twins washed their hair and their sisters bathed them and dried them first with fine white corn meal and then with corn pollen. Then the Sun and his spirit wife went to the eastern room and brought sweet-smelling flowers with which they rubbed the twins. And they were made beautiful and looked just like the other children of the Sun. And they sat down on a turquoise bench. The Sun Spirit told his daughters to feed the twins and they gave them Yolthkai-tahn (corn meal mush, ceremonially called White-Shell-Food).

The Sun Spirit then asked the twins: "Why did you come to me?" And they answered: "There are monsters killing all of our people and we want to be able to kill them." The Sun Spirit did not answer but took the boys to the east room which was reached by steps. He opened the door, and there they saw many rainbows, and the Sun Spirit asked the twins if that was what they wanted, but the boys said: "No, we do not want that sort of thing." Then the Sun took them to a door at the south and opened it, and there were many plants, corn, beans, and so forth. And the Sun Spirit said: "Is that what you wanted?" The boys said: "No." So the west door was opened, and there they saw clothing and jewelry, and the Sun asked them: "Did you come for this sort of thing?" And they said: "No;" but the boys had forgotten what they wanted and the Sun then showed them many more things.

Then Niltche-beyazh, the Spirit Wind, spoke in their ears and said: "Begochiddy told you to ask for flint armor and the other weapons." So they said to the Sun: "We want the flint armor and the stone knife, lightning arrows, cyclones, hail, and the magic kehtahn." The Sun said to them: "What do you want them for? They are dangerous." And they answered: "We want to dress in that armor and use the weapons to kill the giants and the monsters." When the twins answered thus, the Sun Spirit sat down with his head in his hands and said sadly: "You must not kill your brother," for he claimed the giants as his children. But finally he decided to grant their request and said: "Very well, I will give what you have asked for." And he taught them how to wear the armor, and how to shoot the lightning arrows, and how to use the stone knife, the big hail, the cyclones, and also how to use the magic kehtahn. And they then told him how they were going to kill the monsters, the bears, and other creatures who were harming the people.

49

Then the Sun Spirit gave them the gifts that they had asked for and they started to go back to Tsoll-tsilth on the clouds, the Sun accompanying them. And when they reached there, they rested above the mountain sitting on the clouds, and the Sun Spirit asked them many questions to test their cleverness. He pointed to Siss-nah-jini and asked them its name and the boys answered correctly. The Sun asked the names of all the mountains and they named them correctly. He also pointed to Huerfano Peak below and the boys recognized their home, so the Sun was satisfied that they were intelligent and asked them no more questions.

Killing of the Giant

They were preparing to go to kill the monsters, but the Sun Spirit said to them: "Let me try first to kill the giant." The twins descended on the lightning to the earth at Bahkse-hotetsa, which is near Tsoll-tsilth (Mount Taylor), and then went up to the top of the mountain, carried by the lightning and the rainbow. They sat down on a rock called Azeth which is just south of Mount Taylor (near Grants, New Mexico), and the Wind Spirit told them to hurry and put on their stone armor, so they put it on, and when they had done so, suddenly to the east they saw the giant's forehead appearing, then he passed out of sight again. Then he appeared at the south, then at the west, then at the north, and each time they saw him more plainly until, when he appeared at the north, they could see the whole of him except his feet, and then he disappeared in a flash and went back to his spring, Toh-sit-toh, where he stopped to drink, his hands on the ground.

The boys mounted the magic lightning and rainbow and flew over the giant as he drank, and he saw their reflections in the spring and rose up. They approached from the east and the giant said: "What fine boys, I must have them." They answered together: "What a big giant, we must have him." This enraged the giant and he seized his stone knife and threw it at the boys. It passed under them because the Wind Spirit had warned them, and they rose on the rainbow as the giant threw the knife. When the knife hit the ground, the boys seized it and went around to the south of the giant, and as they came towards him from that direction, the Wind Spirit warned them to bend down, while another stone knife, thrown by the giant, flew over their heads. They picked up this knife also, and went to attack him from the west. The giant threw another knife at them, but, warned by the Wind Spirit, they escaped it by rising into the air, and they picked up that knife. Then they were attacked from the north, and escaped again, and picked up that knife also.

Now the Sun sent help in the form of a big black cloud which dropped down on the giant bringing a black cyclone. And lightning came from the cloud, and broke the giant's suit of stone armor on all four sides, and Hashjeshjin (the Fire God), who was still in the Third World, sent up a volcano with fire coming out of it to help the twins. And the giant shook all over.

Then the twins took their lightning arrows and shot them through the giant, and the arrows threw the giant's heart to a place northeast of Bluewater, and it is still to be seen there in the form of a big black volcanic rock.

From the place where his heart and body fell, the blood started running in rivers in different directions, so the twins drew a line with their stone knife through the blood and made a deep valley to divide the blood streams, for if they should join, the giant would live again; and where the blood settled is now a plain of volcanic rock.

The boys scalped the giant, and took the sinew from the back of his neck and they cut off the point of his heart. Tsoll-tsilth claimed the body and it is still in the mountain. Begochiddy appeared then and said: "You have done well," and then he blew on the giant and turned his body and blood to rock.

The twins went back to their home at Tsilth-nah-ot-zilthy (Huerfano Peak), and greeted their mother and the other three women who were there, and all the women danced with joy when they saw the boys come. The name of the dance is Chonoteen. Etsay-Hasteen played the big flute and then he made the wand such as is now used in the N'dah (or Squaw Dance) ceremony. And they carved a wand with a bow symbol on one side, and a scalp symbol on the other side of it. This wand is called Ahralth-tseen now, but it used to be called Ahtsee-des-tseen.

The twins said: "We have killed the giant, Mother," and she answered them: "Oh, no, you could not have killed such an enormous giant, he has stone clothing and so many knives that you could not hurt him." (Their mother really knew that they had killed the giant, but pretended that she did not). Next morning they had their breakfast, and then they placed in the middle of the hogahn the white cloud with the male rain (heavy rain), also the cyclone, also the hail, and the burning kehtahn. And Nayenezgani, the older twin, said to the younger: "I am going to kill the monsters, meanwhile you must watch this burning kehtahn, and when I am in great danger it will burn very bright and fast; then you must come and help me at once."

Then Nayenezgani asked: "Where shall I find Dah-il-kadeh?" (the great monster that looks like a gopher). And he was told that it lived at Black Lake, so he set off to kill it, and when he walked the ground trembled under his feet he was so powerful, and he carried the fire stick, Nestrahnihi.

Killing of Dah-Il-Kadeh

The monster was watching in all directions and also was guarded by twelve antelopes, but they could not see Nayenezgani because he was flying on the rainbow, and he landed near the monster, and walked around to discover some place from which he could attack it. As he went along, he met the Gopher, who ran back into his hole, then came out again, and kept on running in and out again four times, but finally said to the boy: "What is the matter, my grandson?" And Nayenezgani answered: "I want to kill this monstor, Dah-il-kadeh, but I cannot reach him," and the Gopher said to him, "I am willing to go near him—I am not afraid of him." And the boy said: "If you will help me to reach him, you may have his skin." The Gopher made a hole, and burrowed under the ground to the monster, then he made another hole deeper in the earth, another deeper still, and the fourth tunnel was a very deep one, and was dug under the monster's heart. When the Gopher reached the monster, he ate off the hair under his heart, and the monster felt this and moved, saying: "What is under me?" and the Gopher answered: "I am getting fur to wrap my children who are cold."

Then the Gopher went back to Nayenezgani and told him that he was ready. And they both went into the tunnel, and when they reached the monster's heart and saw it and heard it beating, the boy took a lightning arrow and shot it through the heart. The monster jumped up and destroyed the lower tunnel with his horns, but as he did so the boy ran to the next tunnel, and when the monster destroyed that, the boy escaped to the third tunnel, and when this was destroyed, he hid in the upper tunnel and the monster tore up half of the tunnel in which the boy was hidden, but fell over dead before he could reach the boy.

The antelope guards were rushing around the monster looking for Nayenezgani and when they saw him, he lit some cedar bark with his fire stick and threw a piece to the east and all the antelopes ran after it, then he threw another burning piece of bark to the south, and they ran after that, and another to the west, and another piece to the north. When they had chased after that they were so tired that they were helpless and the boy took his stone knife and killed all but two of them, and he told these two antelopes that they must behave better in the future. He told them this four times, and they agreed that they would be good.

Nayenezgani was still afraid to go near the monster and the Gopher said: "I will find out if he is dead. I will run around on his horns." So he ran from one horn to the other and proved that the monster was dead. And Nayenezgani went up to him and scalped him, and took the sinews of the legs and neck, and took his stomach and filled it with blood. Also he cut off his horns which were the shape of the antelope horns. Though he was very large the monster had a very small eye. Nayenezgani told the Gopher that he could help himself to the rest of the monster, and the Gopher brushed himself with the blood, making himself look so much like the monster that when you look at the Gopher now you can tell how the Dah-il-kadeh looked.

Nayenezgani went home, and as he came near he gave the god-call, Yo-ho-ho-ho and also Ya-ha-ha-ha, and his mother and the other women met him with dancing. Etsay-Hasteen played his flute and they sang. They hung the scalp of the Dah-il-kadeh on the cedar wand, Aralth-tseen, and as they did so, the wand threw off sparks. Then Nayenezgani told his mother about his adventures, and she pretended as before that he could not have killed the monster, but he convinced her that it was true, and he spent the night there.

Killing of the Great Bird

Next day he clothed himself in stone armor and asked his mother and grandmother where he could find the Great Bird, Tseh-nah-hahleh. And his mother told him that it was very dangerous to hunt the bird. Nayenezgani, however, started on his way, taking with him the skin of the Dah-il-kadeh, and the blood enclosed in the monster's stomach, and the earth shook as he went. The rainbow carried him towards the home of the Great Bird on top of Ship Rock. Before he reached it, he dressed himself in the skin of the Dah-il-kadeh, and he carried the monster's stomach full of blood inside his clothing. The Great Bird saw him coming, and flew towards him making much noise, flying over him four times. Then she caught up Nayenezgani in her claws and carried him to Ship Rock, circling it four times and then threw him down between the two peaks. Nayenezgani would have been killed by the fall except for the fact that the feather which the Spider Woman had given him enabled him to fall slowly.

When he lit on the rock, he tore open the stomach full of blood, and the Great Bird thought she had killed him, and so flew off the nest telling her little ones to eat Nayenezgani, as he was dead. Nayenezgani lay still, and the little birds came nearer to him, but he said: "Sh-sh," and frightened them away. They called out to their mother: "Shemah (Mother), this human being is not dead, for he said 'Sh-sh' to us," but the Great Bird said: "That is nonsense, go on and eat. The noise you heard was the sound of his fall." So the Great Bird flew away to the west over the mountains and when she had gone Nayenezgani got up and went to their nest and called the little birds to him, and they were frightened and went back to their nest and began to cry. Nayenezgani told them to be quiet, and that if they made a noise, he would kill them.

The oldest bird came to him and Nayenezgani took hold of him and pushed his beak down, and made his wings a different shape, and painted his wings and tail white and told him to go south and live there and be good, and not do any harm to any one any more, and he became the first eagle. Nayenezgani called the smaller bird to him four times before he would come, and then Nayenezgani gave him a long pair of ears and told him that he was to be the owl, and that if he harmed the earth people he would kill him. And he sent him north to the La Plata Mountains to a place which was to be his home, called Saltahn-iskai, near Pagosa Peak. And the owl was very tired when he reached his new home.

Nayenezgani looked about to find a place in which to hide so that he could kill the parent birds, but the only place he could find was in the nest, and so he hid there. Then the male rain started, and he saw the father bird flying back with something in his claws and when he came nearer, Nayenezgani saw that he was carrying a handsome young man who was dressed in fine jewelry and many bracelets. And the bird dropped the man, and when he fell the turquoise jewelry flew in every direction. The father bird then lit on the peak, but before he folded his wings, Nayenezgani shot him and saw that the young man whom the bird had dropped on the peak was a Taos Indian. From the west began a light female rain, and the mother bird flew in, carrying a young and pretty girl dressed in white shell beads. And she dropped the girl on the rock. Just as the mother bird lit on the peak, Nayenezgani shot her with a lightning arrow and the bird fell dead from the peak.

Nayenezgani now looked about to find a way down from the peak, and below he saw a bat whose name was Jahbunny-estsan (Bat Woman), and he said to her: "Grandmother, help me down, and I will give you a feather." She hid four times and would not answer. Finally she told him to go to the other side of the peak, and then she appeared to Nayenezgani with a basket on her back, upheld by spider webs. She danced about when she reached the top of the peak and said to him: "Now get into my basket," but Nayenezgani answered: "The strings are too small, they will break under my weight," but she said: "No, I can carry very heavy load with these webs."

Nayenezgani was afraid and would not get into the basket, so the Bat Woman told him to fill it with big rocks and he did so, and the strings of the spider web still held, although they buzzed with the strain. Nayenezgani was convinced that the Bat Woman could carry him, and he took the stones out of the basket, and went over to the edge of the peak and got into the basket. The Bat Woman told him to shut his eyes, and she began to go down. Half way down the Bat woman stopped on a small ledge and walked back and forth while Nayenezgani wondered whether they were on the ground or not, but he could not see as she had told him to keep his eyes shut.

He grew so nervous that he opened his eyes, and at once they both fell to the ground, but fortunately the shelf on which they had been was not far up the cliff. The Bat Woman was so angry that she struck Nayenezgani with a cane she held in her hand, because he had opened his eyes. Then he got out of the basket and went to where the Great Bird had fallen. He pulled out twelve of his tail feathers, doing the same to the female bird, and he scalped both birds with his stone knife, and told the Bat Woman to help herself to the feathers that remained, and she filled her basket with small feathers.

Nayenezgani warned her not to go through the sunflower place as she would regret it; and he set off towards home, but as he went, he watched the Bat Woman because he saw she was going straight to the sunflower place. When she reached there, all the feathers in the basket blew out, and she lost them all. She went back to find the dead birds again, thinking that she would find more feathers, but Nayenezgani did not wait to see if she got any. He mounted his rainbow and went home, where his return was celebrated in the same way as it had been before.

Destruction of the Kicking Rock

Next day after breakfast, having found out from his mother where he

54

should go, he started off to Tseh-ed-ah-eh-delkithly (the Rock-that-Kicks-People-into-the-River). He saw a man lying on his back with his head on a bluff and his feet near the river, and he was pulling the whiskers out of his chin. When Nayenezgani tried to pass, he kicked at him, and Nayenezgani said: "What is the matter, Sechai (Grandfather)?" The Rock Man said: "My leg was cramped, and I had to kick to straighten it out." Four times he was questioned and he answered four times. After that Nayenezgani took his stone knife and hit the Rock Man on the head, and cut through his breast, hips and legs, chopping him into four pieces and then scalping him.

The Rock Man's children lived in the river and Nayenezgani threw the pieces of the Rock Man down to them, and heard them quarreling for the pieces of meat, saying: "That is my piece," not knowing that they were eating their own father. Then Nayenezgani went down into the river and killed all the children except two. One was called Kahtsen (Alligator) and Nayenezgani said to him: "You must never hurt anyone again, will you promise this?" And the alligator answered: "I am not sure." Nayenezgani asked this four times but the alligator would not promise. The other child who was spared was called Siss-'tyel (Turtle), and was told to be good in the future, as he would be used for medicine by men, and his shell would be used to drink out of and also to make medicine in, and the turtle agreed to this and said that he would always be good. So Nayenezgani went home on the rainbow and they danced and celebrated his return as before.

Destruction of Rolling Rock

The next morning Nayenezgani asked where he would find Tseh-ehi (the Rolling-Rock) and his mother told him that it was in the Jemez Mountains, so he went there and looked at it from a peak near by. When Nayenezgani tried to approach it, the Rock began to roll towards him and he shot his lightning arrow at the Rock from the east, but could not hit it, and the Rock then rolled back to its den. Then Nayenezgani shot at it from the south and managed to knock a little splinter from it while the Rock pursued him. He then approached the Rock from the west and the same thing happened, and also from the north, and at the end he only managed to knock off a few pieces and could not injure it, and meanwhile it kept chasing him while he was barely able to avoid it.

At his home at Huerfano the magic kehtahn began to burn very brightly, which showed that Nayenezgani was in great danger. So they sent hail, big rain, and cyclones to attack the Rock. And the water soaked it, and Hashjeshjin burnt it with his fire, and then hit it with a stone knife, and large pieces were broken off it. The Rock tried to escape them, but they chased it into a mountain from which it burst out as though from a volcano, and finally they chased the Rock four times around the earth, while it grew smaller and smaller, until at last it fell into the Grand Canyon, where it now is. After taking its scalp the three went home—Nayenezgani and Hashjeshjin with Mah-ih-degishi (Spirit of the Scalp).

Destruction of Staring-Eyes-That-Kill

The next hunting by Nayenezgani was of the monsters called Benan-yah-runi (Staring-Eyes-That-Kill), who lived at Tsilth-lachee, Red Mountain.

Asheen-assun, the Salt Woman, brought Nayenezgani a lump of salt, and told him how to use it in killing these monsters. And she told him to take his fire sticks also. As he came near where the Staring-Eyes-That-Kill lived, he found a great many of their tracks, and followed them to where they lived in a cave, and they all stared at him, never closing their eyes. Nayenezgani made a fire with his fire sticks and threw a handful of salt into the fire, which exploded into the monsters' eyes, blinding them, and they had to shut their eyes to rub the salt and fire out of them. Then Nayenezgani took his stone knife and killed them all, except two which crept into a little crack in the wall of the cave. One of these he made into a Screech Owl, Gloutrah-nasjah, and the other he called Nah-zunni, Snow Bug. He told both of these never to harm people any more and they agreed. And he sent the Screech Owl to the prairies, where he was to live in a hollow in the ground. And he sent the Snow Bug to travel on the snow in the winter forever. Then he went home again, and they celebrated in the same way with dancing and song. He told them how he had killed all of the Staring-Eyes-That-Kill. Every time he returned home he hung the scalps of the monsters he had killed on the scalp stick.

Destruction of Great Centipedes

After breakfast the next morning, he started out to kill the Sil-dil-hushy-tso (Great Centipedes), and they told him that they lived at a place called Tseh-negleen (Water-Meeting-Place) on the La Plata River near Farmington.

So he went there and found a lot of centipedes who, as they walked, bowed themselves up in the middle, and then could spring a great distance to catch their victims. The largest centipede jumped at Nayenezgani but could not bite through the stone armor, and Nayenezgani seized his stone knife, and cut him into little pieces, and then killed all the rest of them and their little ones except a pair, a male and a female, and these he let go, telling them to behave themselves and never harm anyone. He scalped the largest centipede and went home, where he hung the scalp on the scalp stick, and they held the usual celebration.

Destruction of Crushing Rocks

The next morning he went to Chustoh-ba-ahd, south of Taos, where he wanted to destroy the Crushing Rocks, Tseh-ah-kindithly. And he rode on his Rainbow and took with him the horns of the Dah-il-kadeh. When the Rocks tried to crush him, he would evade them on his Rainbow and the Rocks could not crush him. He did this four times, and then he took the horns of the Dah-il-kadeh and put them across between the Rocks which prevented them from coming together. He then threw his fire between the Rocks, and heated them so hot that when he hit them with his stone knife, they splintered into many pieces. Before he left, he motioned toward the splintered rocks and said: "Hereafter you will be used for the colored sands of which our sandpaintings will be made." And this colored rock which Nayenezgani burned is what the Indians now use for their paintings. Then he went home and was received with rejoicing.

Destruction of Cutting Reeds and Other Monsters

The next morning after breakfast he went to destroy the Cutting Reeds, Luka-degizh, which were at Toh-gay-tyelth, a round peak west of Taos. He took with him his fire sticks and when he came to the little canyon where the Reeds lived, he pretended to enter on one of the many trails, and the Reeds tried to catch him, waving and clashing together, but four times they missed him. When he tried to cut the Reeds down with his stone knife, he found it was impossible, so he used his fire sticks and burned them all up except two. These he cautioned to be good in the future and he told them that the earth people would use them in their ceremonies. The two Reeds agreed to this, and Nayenezgani took the scalp from the largest Reed and went home and told his mother that he had burned all the Cutting Reeds, and then they celebrated.

Then he went to destroy the Canyon-that-Spreads-Apart, Tseh-ko, which is also near Taos. Four times he avoided being dropped into the Canyon as it spread, and then he put four obsidian stones across it, and fastened them together to hold the Canyon steady. He told the Canyon that it must be good and not engulf people, and that the earth people would use it in their ceremonies. And the Indians pray now to this Canyon. He then went home and they celebrated as before.

The next day he went to destroy the Cactus-that-Catches, Hoosh-entsah-etso, which grew at Siss-pai (near Canjilon). And he destroyed the Cactus with his stone knife, and burned all except the little ones which he preserved. And he told them to be good, and that they would be used in the ceremonies. Then he went home to his mother.

Next he went to kill the bad Rock Swallows, Tush-gizhi-ent-dilkizhi, who lived near the Mancos River in one of the canyons near Mesa Verde. When Nayenezgani went into this canyon the birds swooped down on him, and he shot his lightning arrows at them, but could not hit them, as they flew too quickly. Then they tried to hurt him, but his stone armor protected him. At home, at Huerfano, the magic kehtahn began to burn brightly, warning Tohbachischin. And he blew four times toward his brother. And the cyclones, hail, thunder, and also the white cloud on which Tohbachischin usually rode, all went to help Nayenezgani.

Meanwhile Nayenezgani was running from the birds, who followed him in clouds like a swarm of bees. Then rain came from the white cloud, and the cyclones swept the birds aside, and the hail stones struck them so all were killed except two little ones. Nayenezgani told these two little birds to be good and do no harm, and the birds promised to do so. So the God let them live in the Canyon peacefully. Then Nayenezgani went home and they celebrated.

Next Nayenezgani went to find the Bears-that-Trail, Shush-nah-Kahi. There were four of these bears, and they lived on a mountain called Tsilth-entsah, near the Blanco River about four miles east of Farmington. When the god came there and went up the mountain, he met a strange-looking girl named Shikinh-shush-nah-tlehay (Changing-Bear-Maiden), who had red eyes, and carried a basket full of berries on her back. Nayenezgani asked her where she came from and she replied: "I have been picking berries in the canyon and there are many still there." Nayenezgani went on, and suddenly he saw the Bears coming towards him in single file. He immediately mounted his rainbow and rose into the air, and when he had gone up about fifteen feet, the Bears rushed under him trying to grasp his shadow. Nayenezgani then took his lightning arrows and killed them all.

The girl he had met on the way was a Bear in human form, and now she appeared coming up the canyon in her Bear form, and Nayenezgani killed her also. He then scalped the four Bears but not the Girl Bear. He dragged her down the canyon to a big piñon tree, and spread her arms and legs far apart, put his head down close to hers and said: "I will bring you back to life if you will promise not to harm people any more." The Bear Maiden did not answer, but Nayenezgani blew four times on her head, and suddenly she came to life, sprang up and ran away to the mountains. Then Nayenezgani went home and they celebrated as before.

After that he asked his mother if there were any more monsters to be killed and she answered: "No, you have killed them all, there are no more left." Nayenezgani was not sure that this was true, so he started out and visited all the mountains in the east looking for monsters, but he found none, and after that he went to the mountains of the south, west, and north but found no more monsters to kill, so he came home again.

One evening after this, while sitting outside his hogahn, he saw a great red light to the north, and this made him angry and he said to the people: "You said there were no more monsters to kill but there must be some over there." And he brought the people out of the hogahn and they all saw the red light. Nayenezgani then took a forked stick and stuck it in the ground and aimed it at the fire so that in the morning he would be able to tell where the fire was. The next day he looked along the stick, and marked the place on the distant mountain to which the stick pointed before starting out, and then he mounted his rainbow and went there.

The place where the fire had been was at the La Plata River and Nayenezgani found there an old woman, Sahn, who was Old Age. She was

58

sleeping near a fire, while on the other side of the fire slept a black man, Bi-eth, which means Lazy Man or Sleepy-Man-of-no-Account. Nayenezgani raised his stone knife to kill the woman, but as he did so he fell asleep, and dropped down on the ground next to her. The old woman waked up when he fell and said: "What is the matter, why do you try to kill me, Grandson?" And then she waked up Nayenezgani. Other people now came towards them. They were Yah (Body Lice), Dechin (Hunger), Tayen (Thinness), and Ahtsay-lin (Lies). Old Age begged Nayenezgani to spare her; she said she would hurt no one, and that some people would love to be as old as she was. Bi-eth, or Sleepiness, also begged Nayenezgani not to kill him, as sleep is always good for people. Yah, Body Lice, also begged for mercy and said: "I am good-natured, let me go." Tayen, Thinness, begged for his life and said: "Thinness usually hurts no one." Dechini, Hunger, begged for mercy, saying: "If you starve a little, you enjoy your food much more afterwards"

So Nayenezgani let them all go free, and he told the four—Hunger, Lice, Thinness, and Sleepiness—to go and stay at Tseh-dokohe, nine miles north of Farmington; and Old Age and Lies were to go to a place fifteen miles east of Pueblo Bonito, named Yath-pai. Then Nayenezgani went home again as there were some Yehtso-lapai (Gray Giants) wandering about. And Nayenezgani surrounded them and left them at the spring of Tchah-toh near Huerfano and turned them into stones. Begochiddy came down again from heaven and they told him about the killing of the monsters and he was very glad and said to them: "I will be back in twelve days and we will have a Council."

Plans for Flood and Recreation

At the end of twelve days, Hashjeshjin (The Fire God) and all the gods came and they held a Council in the Hogahn called Hadahonesteen (Mirage). The twins sat on one side of the Hogahn, and the gods on the other and the gods talked very softly as they did not want the twins to hear them. They were talking of making more mountains and of fastening the mountains to-gether with metal nails. The boys grew tired of hearing the whispering of the gods, and wanted to know what they were talking about, and asked them to talk out loud so that they could hear. Their mother said to them: "We were talking of strengthening the mountains and putting them in good condition, and we are planning another flood to wash away all the old plants and trees, and of planting new ones, and of fastening the mountains down with metal, so that they will not be washed away in the flood." She said that the gods were glad that the bad monsters were killed and that they wanted to cleanse and recreate the world, and the twins agreed that this should be done.

So they began to fasten the mountains down with lead, gold and so forth. And they worked seven days strengthening the mountains. Each mountain was strengthened and made in small size, but when Begochiddy used the Ethkaynah-ashi and blew at the mountains four times, they grew bigger and better than they were before. Then they killed all the trees because they

59

thought them bad, and Begochiddy said that after seven days it would begin to rain. And all the gods went into the big bamboo flute again.

And the rain began and kept on for forty-two days, and water covered the whole earth except the tops of the mountains. When it stopped, a great rainbow appeared over the world, and on top of it stood Begochiddy with his hands spread out in gladness.

The water covered the world for forty-two days, and then began to decrease and run off in different directions, leaving only mountains and rocks, and no plants or animals. The gods came back to Huerfano Peak where they had lived before, and Begochiddy waved his hands over the world, and at once it was covered with trees and plants and animals, and when it had rained a little, everything began to grow. The gods planted a little cornfield called Dah-gejol-gishy at Huerfano. They also grew their squash, beans, and tobacco there. They named the mountains again and also named some other places, Bezh-lachee-begizh—Washington Pass over the Chuskai Mountains; Tseh-hatral—volcanic rocks near the foot of the pass over the Chuskai Mountains; also Sontso-lah Mountain which is near Crystal, New Mexico; Tsentyel—Flat Rock in Canyon de Chelly; also Nashjeh-tseel—Spider Mountain or Peaked Rock in Canyon de Chelly; Toh-deh-hashkeh—on top of Black Mountain near Chin Lee; Ahdah-tintsoi—peak on Black Mountain; Nah-tee-tseel—Tobacco Mountain near Bluff City; Tsilth-kay-hozhoni—Beautiful Mountain north of Chuskai Mountain; Ahgeh-naschini—Crown Point; Tsis-kit—Cedar-Covered Flat-Topped Rock near Ojo Alamo. They visited these places as they named them and then went back to Huerfano.

Then they met again in the hogahn for a Council with the boys sitting on one side and the gods on the other as before. And as before the twins could not hear, and asked after a time what the gods were talking about. Their mother said: "We are planning to make more people to fill this fine new world," and the boys were very glad to hear this. They discussed how the people were to be made, and decided to make the men of turquoise and white corn, and the women of white shell and yellow corn, and the corn pollen would be for the male and the corn bug for the female. The gods took these six things and turned them into three men and three women.

Begochiddy said: "I am going to a place called Siss-nah-tyel, which is near Kim-beto where Kay-des-tizhi, the Man-Wrapped-in-a-Rainbow lives. And I am going to plan to make animals there, and I shall make the donkey first, Tahilth-sapai, which means Dusty Beast because he is always rolling in ashes, then the sheep, then the horses and after that all sorts of animals. And Begochiddy laughed as he was planning these animals and he kept going back and forth between Siss-nah-jini, which was his home, and the Council.

Creation of Man and Animals

Then they began to make Man. They made his feet and his toe nails and his ankles of soil of the Earth, his legs of lightning, his knees of white shell and

60

his body of white corn and yellow corn. His veins were of striped corn and blue corn, the calico corn made the hair on his arms and body, the black corn made his eyebrows, and the red corn was his blood. His heart was of obsidian, and his breath was the white wind; his ear was made of white shell and the ear drum of mica. They took all the flesh of all the different animals to make his body, and also all other kinds of flower pollen. They made him of all kinds of water: rains, springs, lakes, rivers and ponds, also of the black cloud and the male rain, and the sky, and the female rain, and they made his arms of the rainbow. His hair was made of darkness, his skull of the sun, his whiskers of darkness and his face of daybreak. His nose was made of Yohlachee (red beads), his eyes of the Suns, his teeth of white corn and his speech of thunder, his tongue of straight lightning, and the little whirlwind was what kept his nerves moving. The movement of his finger was the air, his saliva was the little rain, and the water of his nose and his tears were the medium rain; and his food was of white and yellow corn. And the name of the new kind of human being was Anlthtahn-nah-olyah, meaning Created-from-Everything. The people who had been in the cave were called Hahjeenah-dinneh, which means The-People-Who-Came-Up.

Hashje-altye (Talking God) was the first to be made, then Hashje-hogahn (House God), next Nahtahn-lakai-eshki (White Corn Boy), then Nahtahn-tsoi-atehd (Yellow Corn Girl), then Tradadeen-eshki (Corn Pollen Boy), then Tradadeen-atehd (Corn Pollen Girl), Sahanahray-eshki (the Holy Spirit Boy), and Bikay-hozhon-atehd (Holy Spirit Girl). These were the first human beings made on this earth of the substance of the universe which already was full of the Holy Spirit.

They made animals, and the donkey was made first of a substance called Ne-ho-pah, and his hoofs were made of obsidian.

This is the way they made men and creatures: they put everything which was used to make man laid out in pairs in a line on the Robe of Daybreak at the south, west, and north sides of the hogahn and covered them with a buckskin. And the pair on the north side was covered with a rainbow as well as a buckskin. At the east side were the Yeh gods. The spirit of Siss-nah-jini Mountain motioned with a rainbow over all the human beings, and the Spirit of Tsoll-tsilth Mountain motioned over them with the sunlight, and they sang all night over the people, and blessed them with the light and the rainbow, and towards daybreak they took medicine and herbs and sprinkled over the human beings, and then the Yeh motioned over them with the Ethkaynah-ashi, and power came to them, and they were shaken with it.

The gods gave strong power to the people and covered them with flowers. And also they covered the new animals with plants and grasses; and then all the gods spoke and told the people four times to rise, that day had come. Then the Yeh took off the buckskins which had covered the people and the animals and Hashje-hogahn, the house God, gave his cry: Ah-ho-ah-ho. And the Yehs' spirits went in the four directions into the four Holy Mountains, and when the spirits entered the north mountain, the bird spirits went with them. The four mountains were called Siss-nah-jini, Tsoll-tsilth, Do-go-slee-ed, and Debeh-entsah. If people do not believe that the Yeh spirits are in these mountains and keep them holy, sickness and disease will come to afflict the people, for the Yehs control sickness (and that is the reason why the Indians are not healthy now, because at the ceremonies they do not take these things seriously).

Then the newly-made people, Anlthtahn-nah-olyah, arose and the gods motioned towards them with the Ethkay-nah-ashi and the new people spoke, saying: "Shemah (mother), Lecheh (father)," for they saw Begochiddy and called him father, and they called Estsan-ah-tlehay their mother. Then the new people ate some white corn, for, although they were made of corn, it was good for them to eat it, and the Navajos live on corn today.

First Song of The Hogahn

This ends the creating of human beings and creatures, and Begochiddy was glad and laughing when he had finished the creation. [6] And he made the new people run races around the world, and the animals raced too, and the donkey won, for Begochiddy loved him most, and the mule came in second. They then made a hogahn for the new people, and at present the hogahn song, Hogahn-beyin, is sung just after sundown for thanksgiving and as a prayer. Natah-hogahn-beyin is said.

After this Begochiddy turned all the animals loose to wander as they pleased, but the donkey was kept for his own use; and he said to the animals: "Some day I will come back and need you, but now you can wander as you please." There were a great many songs sung while he was making the animals and there are so many of these songs that today very often not all of the songs are sung in one night's ceremony.

They gathered for another Council in the hogahn and again the gods spoke so low that Nayenezgani and his brother, Tohbachischin, could not hear what they said, and the twins asked the gods to speak so that they could understand them and the gods answered: "We were talking about the creating of animals and human beings, and how you killed the monsters. Now we are planning to go and get the people (Hahjeenah-dinneh) who are living in the cave." Nayenezgani said: "That is well."

Then they made a great rainbow shaped like a basin, and they all mounted this and went to the cave. They asked Nayenezgani and his brother to go, but Etsay-hashkeh, the Coyote, stayed behind as he did not care to go, and the other gods did not urge him.

While the gods were gone on the journey to the cave, the Coyote made some little coyotes of his own, a white one from the east, a yellow one from the west which was a female, a blue one from the south which was a male, and a black coyote from the north which was a female, and each pair stood nose to nose; and he also made a dog which stood with the female black coyote. The names of these coyotes were: the east, Ki-othkath-tee-ni-gosai, which means Turning-in-the-Daybreak; west, Nahotsoi-nah-go-sai, which means Turning-in-the-Afterglow; south, Chadidoth-dani-gosai, which means Turning-in-the-Darkness; and the name of the dog was Dobinny-des-daha, or Trailing Dog. Etsay-hashkeh also made some crazy coyotes. If one of these should bite a human being, he would probably go mad. And also he made some mad dogs whose bites would bring madness.

Etsay-hashkeh made these creatures because he did not know how to behave, and no one was there to know what he was doing. And though Begochiddy knew what the Coyote was doing he was willing that these animals should be made.

Return of Created Beings from Cave

Meanwhile the gods reached the cave, and they had to use ladders to reach down to the Hahjeenah-dinneh or Emergence People and bring them up to the surface of the earth. So the people came out onto this earth, and were very glad to leave the cave as they had been there a long time, and had been much worried about what was going to become of them. The little ants were the first to come out, and the turkey people were the last, and Hashjeshjin (the Fire God) counted them as they came out.

The gods told them that they had made a beautiful world and that it was quite safe and they answered: "We are glad." Begochiddy then said to the gods that all people in the future should have different languages and the gods agreed to this. They divided all the clothing so that each people should have a certain share, and the beasts also could choose which tribe they should join. The Navajos took the best seed of the corn while the Pueblos and Zuni took the poorer seeds. The birds chose their tribes, but only the turkey people chose to go with the Navajos. Estsan-ah-tlehay, the Changing-Woman, took the turkeys and held them in her arms.

Begochiddy and the gods said to the people: "You are all going to have different languages now, live differently, and do your hair in different ways." The Navajos did their hair in a queue and the other tribes cut their hair across the front, and this is the way they do it to this day. They told the birds how they were to live and build their nests and they all agreed to do as they were told. Then Begochiddy told the people how they were to worship. They must keep the prayer stick or ceremonial Kehtahns holy, and they must place pollen and flint and shell beads and turquoise and medicine near the kehtahns when they pray, and Begochiddy will hear them and answer their prayers.

Separation of People into Clans

Begochiddy said to the plants and the trees: "You must grow and blossom and bear fruit at certain seasons." And they agreed to do this. Then he said to all creatures: "After four days you can go wherever you please." And when that time was ended, Begochiddy blew four times in different directions and some of the Navajos went towards Huerfano, and some went to a place called Nehal-zhini, the Black Place, and some to Kih-ah-ah, the Standing-Up-Place near Crown Point. And the people who were last to be made, the Anlthtahn-nah-olyah, went to live near Huerfano, and never went far away from it. This clan family was then named Tsilth-bin-jodithy, which means Wandering-Around-the-Mountain. They are now called the Asheen or Salt Clan.

They made a ceremonial hogahn in which the gods told stories of the third world; and this story and the songs of the Creation were handed down from these chieftains to the people and then from one generation to another, and so it has been handed down to this day. Nayenezgani was made the commander of the earth as Begochiddy was in heaven. They learned the Yeh ceremony, Tseh-rahd-n'dinneh, at this time.

To make the four chiefs holy, they put earth from all the holy mountains into their shoes, and they put rock crystals into their mouths so as to make all that they said true.

After a time, the Salt Clan, Asheen, increased and spread to other places where they made homes and these made the different clans which now exist; and the people who stayed at Huerfano are called Hogahn Clan. Begochiddy told the people: "As I have made each clan and each building, I have made for each a different spirit and I laughed as I made them." And then Begochiddy made two other spirits known as Bego-zhini and Bego-tso, and these no one has seen.

The Sun said to Estsan-ah-tlehay: "I want you to go to a place in the west where I can visit you now and then." And she said she was willing to go. The Sun told her to tell the gods that she was going and find out whether they would agree. So she asked them and they said: "No, we will go to the west, but you must go to the east." And she told the Sun what they had said, but he answered: "No, let the others go east, everything is lovely in that direction, but you must go west to the Island" (Santa Cruz, off the coast of Santa Barbara, California). And the Sun told her this four times and said: "Even if the gods do not want you to go to the Island, you must go, and certain gods of the Yeh will go with you and twelve other people. And I will send guards for you: the Hail, Thunder, Lightning, Rain and the Water Monster."

Journey of Estsan-Ah-Tlehay to the West

Then the Sun sent his messenger, Tohnilai, the Dragon Fly, to tell Begochiddy to come down to them, and he came, and they told him about this dispute and asked him what they should do. Then Begochiddy answered: "That is well, Estsan-ah-tlehay must go to the Island." Begochiddy spoke to the other gods about it and the other gods said: "No, we wish to go. Let Estsan-ah-tlehay stay here."

The Coyote, Etsay-hashkeh, said: "I will take some of the last people made, Anlthtahn-nah-olyah, and a dog, and we will go north." So he went north with a man, a woman, and two dogs. And these people never came back. They are now called Dinneh-nahoo-lonai (Eskimo).

They asked the turkeys whether they wanted to go with Estsan-ah-tlehay. The turkeys could not make up their minds, but were going back and forth between the different people. So then they told the turkeys that they must go to Tsoll-tsilth (Mount Taylor), which they finally did.

Estsa-assun, the First Woman, did not want Estsan-ah-tlehay to go away to the west, but the gods said: "It must be so, and she must start in the morning." When morning came, they had the Ceremonial-Before-Traveling. First, Estsan-ah-tlehay made some white shell ceremonial mush, and Estsa-assun made red shell mush. Estsan-ah-tlehay made the mush in a big black pot, and as they stirred the coals under it they said a prayer, and while they stirred it with a pudding stick, they prayed again, raising the stick towards the sky. Then the gods and the twelve people who were going to the west sat down on one side of the hogahn, while those who were opposed to their going sat on the other side. Then the people with Estsan-ah-tlehay ate, rubbing themselves and blessing their food, and praying to be strong and not tired during the journey. Estsa-assun, who made the red shell mush, and the people with her grabbed the food, eating it carelessly, and drinking hot water. They represent the careless people who are angry against the gods, and those who eat in this way bring sickness. The gods who ate the white shell mush ate slowly, praying and behaving properly, which is the ceremony of eating. Estsa-assun told the people that when they increased very much, there would be earthquakes and war between them. Etsay-Hasteen, her husband, said nothing because he could not speak against his wife, but he felt very badly.

Now they started to go, and Hashje-altye (the Talking God) stood in front of the people facing east and all the people had flowers in their hands and the spirits of the birds were with them. Nayenezgani held the scalp stick in his hand. There is a song about the starting of this journey called Deh-ye-yah-heh, meaning "I am a white shell woman and I am going."

Kai yolthkai estsa chin
Eshli nihai in inyah.

The travellers who were going west with Estsan-ah-tlehay visited all the mountains that have been named, and when they reached the second mountain, Tsoll-tsilth, they saw in the distance the smoke of Estsa-assun and Etsay-Hasteen going on their way to the north with Etsay-hashkeh. Asheen-assun, the Salt Woman, stayed with the Salt Clan at Huerfano.

The travellers with Estsan-ah-tlehay, after making a circuit of the holy mountain, started to go west from Huerfano by Bezh-lachee-begizh (Cottonwood Pass), over the Chuskai mountains. As they passed over it, they touched a big rock which stands there called Tseh-bezh-delneheh. And you

65

can see the hand prints there now, and Indians who pass that way should put their hand on the hand prints and pray.

After that they came to a spring and made balls out of corn meal and ate what they could and left the rest near the spring; these now are turned into rocks like marbles, Tseh-genesh-hize. The Sun came down and ate with them, and near that place is a sign of the Sun on the rock, also the sign of the Moon.

They went then to a cliff with a rock with a hole through it sticking out of the cliff. This place is named Tseh-hatral. They left the Corn Pollen Boy (Tradadeen-eshki) and the Corn Pollen Girl (Tradadeen-etadeh) there to live, and also the Corn Bug Bird (At-atid-ehd).

Then they went on to Sontso-lah, two mountains with a path between them near Crystal, New Mexico. There they left two spirits to live, Siss-yatyeh and Tsilth-deginnih, which are the Echo and Holy Mountain Spirits; and in that place all Navajos should pray.

Then they went down Tseh-gih (Canyon de Chelly) to Tyen-tyel (Flat Rock) and there they left Tseh-atehd-deginnih (Rock Girl People), and also Tseh-altyeh (Echo Rock). Then they went to Nasjeh-tseel (Spider Rock), and came to Tseh-benigeh (a Rock in Canyon de Chelly). They left there Hashje-altye (the Talking God) and Hashje-hogahn (the House God). And at Kin-lakai (White House) they left Hashje-baka and Hashje-ba-ahd, the Male and Female Gods; these are the dancers. All these last places mentioned are in Canyon de Chelly.

They passed by Chin Lee and went to a big rock island in the stream named Tseh-benazelleh, and landed on top of this rock and made some foot prints there. Then they flew from there in a flute to the top of Black Mountain near Toheen-da-hazkah, a flat-topped peak. There they blew their noses and cleaned themselves and left some white rocks in that place. Nayenezgani was carrying the scalp stick and he threw it on to the top of the rock, and said that no Navajo must go up there.

Then they entered the flute again, and went to the Ozheh-be-hogahn, a tribe of the Hopi Indians living north of Moencopi in a very lovely place. And they gave flint to these people, and also a feather of the Great Bird, Tseh-nah-hahleh. [7]

They went in the flute to the top of San Francisco Peak, Dogo-slee-ed, and from there they walked in the afternoon to a little mesa covered with cedar called Tsini-deh-aheh, and they slept there and had a Ceremony and Song. At this Ceremony they made the Gohi-ninny. One of the travellers was turned into a Gohi-ninny, and they made four of these men here who were the ancestors of the Pima tribe.

Then they went on to Tsilth-kai-des-kahli, a white-topped mountain, and left there four people called Delzheh, who are often slaves of the Hopis and were probably the Yuma Indians.

Then they came to Tsilth-nah-tsakai, Half-White-Mountain, and left there four people called Bes-antsai (meaning unknown) then to Tsilth- (an unknown mountain), and left there four people called Belthrah (Apaches); then

66

to Tsilth-deltsoi (Yellow Mountain near Kingman, Arizona), where they left four people called Nah-ketlah-tsi-koi, which is a tribe that wears wooden soles on its shoes.

Then they went to Tsilth-n'doh-kunsh (Sailing Mountain) and left there the tribe called Away-kiyatye, and this tribe talked like babies.

Then they came to Tsilth-dohgeh-jiggah, and left there people called Bekekeh-yazhi (Papagoes) who wear sandals with thongs between their toes. Then they went to Tsilth-beneh-holkoh Mountain, and left there a people called Kah-dinneh, or Arrow People. Then they went to Haltahn-neligay-tseel or Mirage Mountain, and left there a people called Haltahn-ah-begay, or Mirage Clan.

At Foggy Mountain, Hahden-nesteen-tseel, they left the Foggy Clan. And at Nes-teen, which is the Coast Range of California, they left twelve people. Then they mounted on the Fog and rode over a great deal of water to Tsilth-gant-tseel (which is a little peak on Santa Cruz Island off the coast of Santa Barbara, California). After they had landed on the peak, they saw Begochiddy walking towards them on the water. His hair was shining, and little rays of light shone and sparkled from him.

Making of The House of Estsan-Ah-Tlehay on the Island

Then they made a great house of rock crystal which shone and made rainbows as the light reflected from it. And the Wind, and Light, and all of the other spirits helped to make it. It was called Tralth-kageh-bekindeh-nah-elth, or the House-Which-Floats-on-Water. In the east they made a white shell room, in the south a turquoise room, in the west a yellow room made of abalone shell, and in the north a black jet room; and little Suns were placed in it to give light. The house was four stories tall and ladders were made of white shell, jet, turquoise, and abalone to reach the upper stories. At the east they placed a white shell door, at the south a turquoise door, at the west a door of abalone shell, and at the north a door of jet. To close and bar the east door, there was a large white shell stick, and at the north door there was a black thunderbird, Iknee-dithklith. On the top of the house was a many-colored thunderbird, larger than any other, and chief of the thunderbirds, and he carried little thunderbirds on his back.

In the center was a big room and in it an altar decorated with all colors, and Estsan-ah-tlehay danced in front of it while the altar varied from one color to another. At the main door to the east, there was a white medicine rattle which would sound whenever anyone approached. This was the home of Estsan-ah-tlehay, and there is a song about this.

Meanwhile, the Salt Woman, Asheen-assun, who was left at Huerfano, went to the hill near Crystal (New Mexico), wondering where she could make a home. But she did not like it there, so she returned to Huerfano and started out again. She went to Zuni where she wandered about for a while, and made a hole in a big cliff near there, which is still there. The Zunis did not like her very much, but still they did not want her to leave. Then she went to No-hopah, which is near there; and then to Tseh-nihih-deh-ah which is a holy place in the ground south of Zuni, and there she stayed. It is a place where there are two peaks, one of which is female and the other male.

She told all the different tribes to come and visit her occasionally and get salt there. When the people go there and try to get salt, they should dress like Yeh and know a certain song called Asheen-assun-beyin (Salt Woman Song). If they do not know this song, they should sing the song of Estsan-ah-tlehay. Then they must stand in line and say: "Grandmother, come give me some wa-ter," and the water will come rushing in all around them, and then the people can reach down and get the salt. If this song is not sung, the salt grows hard as granite, and no one can get any. This is forever the home of the Salt Wom-an.

Nayenezgani and Tohbachischin came back from the home of Estsan-ah-tlehay and went to where the rivers, the Piedra and the San Juan, meet on the other side of Blanco. They came back in order to teach the Navajos about the ceremonies, and they also took part in the ceremonies, and helped the people and explained the ceremonies to them. The twins went back occasionally to the Island to visit their mother, and stayed four days at a time, and then they came back to their home again.

Creation of More People by Estsan-Ah-Tlehay

Estsan-ah-tlehay, the Changing-Woman, began to be lonely. The mirage made the mountains of the world grow taller, and then she would take a rock crystal and use it as we do a telescope, and she was able to see a great dis-tance; and this she did whenever she was lonely.

She decided to make more human beings to live with her, so she sent word to all the gods to come to her and have a Council. And they came and went into the ceremonial house, the four-colored crystal house on the Island; and the gods stood together on one side and the twins on the other; and Estsan-ah-tlehay said to her boys: "We are going to create more people for I am lonely." The Sun brought down a Turquoise man and a White Shell woman, which were very small—like little images. These were named Doklizhe-eshki, Turquoise Boy, and Yolthkai-etahdeh, White Shell Girl. And the Sun said to the Changing-Woman: "Find out how to make more people like these imag-es."

The Changing Woman bathed herself, and when she had bathed, she rubbed herself on her right side, and with the dead skin which she had rubbed off, she wrapped the little white shell image; and then the Sun rubbed himself on the right side and with the skin that was rubbed off, he wrapped the turquoise image. These small images were the ancestors of the Hushklishni Clan or Mud Clan. Estsan-ah-tlehay and the Sun took the skin from their left sides and with this dead skin they made the Toh-klitsohni or Yellow Water Clan. Estsan-ah-tlehay rubbed herself from her head down to her breast, and with this skin made a female, and the Sun did the same and made a male, and these were called Toh-ah-zholi or Light-Water Clan. Estsan-ah-tlehay took the skin from the back of her head to her hips, and with this made a female, and the Sun did the same, and made a male, and these were called Bitahni Clan. They put a robe of Daybreak over them, and they held a ceremony over them, singing twenty-two verses of a song called Dinneh-noahnai-glah or Making-More-People.

Then Estsan-ah-tlehay took the Rainbow Spirit and moved these people. Then she motioned toward them with Ethkay-nah-ashi which gave them life. And they became human beings. They were created during the night, and at daybreak Estsan-ah-tlehay called four times to them to get up, and they arose and bathed while the people sang over them; and when they came to life they were already twenty-one years old. Estsan-ah-tlehay sang to them, and as she sang, they were clothed in new buckskin shoes and everything needful.

As time went on, the people increased until there were enough to satisfy Estsan-ah-tlehay. There were lots of people, and the children gathered the white shell and broke it up on the beach. Then Estsan-ah-tlehay appointed the chiefs of the clans. The chief of the Toh-klit-sohni, or Yellow Water Clan, was called Nahtal-tilth. Huskah-binah-oltin was the chief of the next clan, Toh-ah-zholi, or Light Water Clan. The chief of the Bitahni Clan was Do-bitsah-hallih. The first chief had a white shell cane, the second had a turquoise cane, the third had an abalone cane, and the fourth a jet cane. There were so many people by this time that Estsan-ah-tlehay sent many of them to another island (Santa Rosa). They were increasing so fast that the children did not thrive, and Estsan-ah-tlehay felt so badly about this that she called a Council to decide what to do. And the gods came together and decided to send many of the people back to a place called Kih-ah-ah near Crownpoint, New Mexico. There is an old ruin on a hill there, and the clan of this place is called Ruin Clan or Kih-ahni. [8]

Journey of the Clans from The Island Back to Navajo Country

Begochiddy said that it was a good idea to send people back to this place and that he would give the different clans protectors on their journey. He appointed the Mountain Lion, Nash-tui-l'tso, as protector to the Mud Clan; and the Bear from Tsilth-dithklith (Black Mountain) was appointed protector of the Yellow Water People, and the Weasel was the guard for the Light Water Clan. The porcupine was the protector for the Bitahni Clan. Then the different guarding animals were brought to the clans, and they held a Council and decided that in four days those who were to go east should start.

They had many riches with them and a great many shells, and their clothing was decorated with shells, while each captain wore a large shell on the top of his head as a sign of his rank. On the day that they were ready to start a fog came up, and in four days they crossed the sea on it and reached the mainland. The travellers, who were called Changing-Woman's-Children, set

69

out walking towards the east, and the Weasel and the Porcupine were carried on the people's backs.

As they journeyed, they came to a place called Tsilth-binny-holoneh, or Mountain-that-Thinks. And in a valley near by they saw a lot of corn fields full of ripe corn, and there they discovered a single hogahn but no people, so all the men put their packs on the ground and walked up to the hogahn. They found no one there, but a fire was burning under a cooking pot filled with deer meat, and they looked around and saw nothing there except that on the east and west walls quivers were hanging, made of mountain lion skin, and on the south and north walls were quivers made of otter skin. Suddenly they heard a sound which came from the quiver made of mountain lion skin, and many men came out of it, young, old and middle-aged, and these were called the Kah-dinneh, or Arrow people. Then from the south side, from the otter skin quiver, came out many women and young girls. So the hogahn was full of the Arrow People and they rejoiced and were glad to see the visitors. The rest of the travellers came up with their packs on their backs and when evening came they all met together and told stories.

The names of the Arrow People and of the travellers were similar, and they all had tobacco. The travellers told their story and told where they were going to, and where they had come from; and the Arrow People said to them: "Estsan-ah-tlehay is our mother, too." And they all made friends as they were all relations.

The Arrow People had plenty of food, and gave the travellers many ears of roasting corn, and then they all went to sleep. The travellers stayed at this place a month, and the Arrow People gave them part of their corn fields, to feed them, and some of the travellers married there. Then the chiefs of the travellers said to one another: "We have stayed long enough in this place, we must move on," and they started on their way, one of the Arrow Women going with them, and they had a lot of corn to eat.

After they had travelled for a while, the chief of the Mud Clan tried to find water by sticking his cane in the ground, but got no water, only mud, and that is the reason why his clan is named the Mud Clan. Then the chief who had the turquoise cane stuck that into the ground and nice blue water gushed out of the ground. The chief who had the abalone shell cane thrust it into the ground but the water that came was salty, and when the jet cane was used, the water that came was black.

Four days after they had left the Arrow People, their Bear Guard began to roar, and then he sang a song called Shonrah-hindeh-hotsil, meaning My-Home-is-in-Danger. When the chiefs heard this song, they called the people together because the Bear had warned them that something was going to happen. Then the Arrow People overtook them suddenly and surrounded them armed with bows and arrows. The Bear ran towards the east and circled around the travellers, biting the Arrow People. And he circled the travellers four times, protecting them from the hostile Arrow People. The next day

70

they started hurriedly without breakfast and travelled on while the Bear came behind to guard them.

A week after this, they were again surrounded by some hostile people called Nakel-astsel-kai (Unknown) early in the morning. The Bear had warned them by growling and singing his song, and the Porcupine threw his spines into the enemy and killed many, and frightened the others so that they ran into the mountains and prayed in fear.

Then they went on again and met a man standing naked with folded arms who was one of the Away-kiyatyeh Clan, the People-Who-Talk-like-Babies. The fourth captain of the travellers took hold of the man and asked him: "Why can't you talk to us?" The Mud Clan, Hush-klishni, and the Bitahni made friends with this naked man and gave him a robe. As they went on their way, they met many tribes and greeted them and passed on. A year passed before they reached Dogo-slee-ed, San Francisco Peaks.

Before they had left the Island, Estsan-ah-tlehay had told them that the holy mountains would bow to them as they went by, and that they must stop and visit the holy mountains. When they came to Dogo-slee-ed, it bowed to them, and they sent one of their people to the top of the mountain who looked southeast and saw in that direction a great white peak (Tsoll-tsilth), and he knew that that was where they were to go next. As he gazed from the peak, the holy mountains rose up, but when he had come down they had sunk again. And he told the people that he had seen where they were to go next, and that he knew the way there.

So they journeyed on, but their guide grew confused and mistook the direction. And they went northeast instead of southeast, and crossed the Little Colorado River, and they were terribly hungry, and so was the Mountain Lion guard who waved his tail. The guide went hunting to try to find food, and the Mountain Lion went out at night and killed many antelope. In the morning the people were fed and stayed there for several days after this. The Lion killed eight antelopes every night for them so that they had plenty of food.

They went on to the north and came to the Painted Desert in the springtime, and they were dying for lack of water, for the four canes of the chiefs could not find any. At length they came to a bluff where there was a cave, and the captains tried to find water with their canes, but only found very little. And the Bear Guard went up to the cave and dug, and dug, and made a spring there, and they called the spring Shush-betoh (Bear Spring). It is near Navajo Mountain, Arizona.

They journeyed on and came to a place near Fort Defiance. Estsan-ah-tlehay had told them to leave the Porcupine on Tsilth-klizhin (Chin Lee Mountain), and they very nearly forgot to do this, but after they had passed the mountain, one of the captains remembered what Estsan-ah-tlehay had told them, and they went back and left the Porcupine on Tsilth-klizhin.

They passed to the north of Chin Lee and found great difficulty there in getting game; even the Mountain Lion Guard could not find any. The Weasel then began to nod, and told them to go to sleep, and while they were sleeping, the Weasel went out and hunted, and the next morning they found that he had killed many rabbits and placed them around the fires, so all the people had plenty to eat, and they thanked the Weasel and patted him.

They went on to Tseh-na-kohni but knew they were going in the wrong direction, so they turned back and went through the Lukachukai Mountains. They travelled by a canyon and as they went the Bear danced, and it is now called the Dancing Canyon.

They came near Toadlena, and then over the plain and "Petrified Wood" Mountain towards Crown Point, and in the gap they heard some people talking about hunting. The people were the Kih-ah-ah Clan or Ruin People and they had a Bear and a Snake to guard them, and when they saw the travellers approach, they took up their bows and arrows, thinking the travellers were enemies.

The Bear Guard of the Kih-ah-ah people, and the Bear who guarded the travellers ran towards each other angrily, and the Big Snake, Kleeshtso, of the Kih-ah-ah Clan, and Nashtui-l'tso, the Mountain Lion, who guarded the travellers, also ran towards each other and started to fight, but as they approached, the bears recognized each other, so that they made friends. When the people saw that their guards were friendly, they all made friends, and the Kih-ah-ah people asked the travellers where they had come from and the travellers learned the name of their hosts.

The travellers said that Estsan-ah-tlehay was their mother and that they had come from her home, and the Kih-ah-ah or Ruin People said: "She is our mother, too," and the chiefs of the travellers and of the Ruin People looked so much alike that they could not be told apart; and their names were almost the same, also their pipes, also their tobacco pouches. The white shell tobacco pouch was decorated with turquoise; the abalone pouch was decorated with jet, and the jet pouch with abalone, and the turquoise pouch with white shell. The first captain's tobacco pouch had a large white shell pipe in it, the second captain's tobacco pouch had a big turquoise pipe in it, the third captain's had an abalone shell pipe in it, and the fourth captain's had a jet pipe in it. And there is a song about these pouches which is called Nahtoh-beyin, Tobacco Song.

Then all the people talked together and visited each other and told stories, and smoked, and had a big feast. The chiefs all made speeches and they asked who had Etsay-entee (a kind of early corn), and the Kih-ah-ah people said: "We have it." They talked a long time about many things and used the playing stone called Espinee, a small stone, and another called Juggie. And they played a game in which they used the following stones: Nezhi, Wonshi, Tsee, Nah-bin-ithbithy, Binskai, Bakaz-tlah, also two stones joined together called Bayez. These are kicking stones. In the game the stone was placed on the foot and kicked; and this game is still played by the Zunis.

Before starting off on their journey again, the travellers were painted with a sign of lightning on their legs, white corn on their breasts, and yellow corn on their backs. And they painted a Sun Dog on each breast and on each shoulder blade. Their faces were painted white. They took food with them, and seed corn, and water in a gourd. They went towards Crown Point and when they came to a place called Teece-sahkahdi, which means Lone Tree, they found a nice level piece of ground and they planted some corn there and this was the cornfield of the Toh-ah-zholi or Light-Water Clan. Then they went to a little hill near Gallup called Sin-nahyah, which means Hill-with-Little-Trees; and they planted corn for the Hushklishni or Mud Clan; and they had a big cornfield and gave the Yellow Water Clan, Toh-klitsohni, one-half of this field.

As the corn began to grow and the little ears were forming, the crows and coyotes began to eat the corn and the people went to their cornfields and lived there to protect the corn. There were some children playing a game in the cornfield; a boy was stationed in the east, a girl at the south, a boy at the west, and a girl at the north, and they were playing a game called Ahchineh-bah-jee-chin which meant: "We won't give the children away." In the game the east boy would run in a circle to touch the girl on the south and then around to all the others hiding in the corn, and if the east boy did not touch one of the children, it would mean that the one he did not touch would be a hunter.

Journey of the Two Children to Estsan-Ah-Tlehay

It began to rain a little, and a rainbow appeared from the north and touched the edge of the cornfield, but the children went on playing and when the east boy had touched the south girl and looked for the west boy and north girl, he could not find them. They hunted a long time for the two children but could not find them, and they went home and told their parents who all rushed out to hunt for the two who were lost. Suddenly the people saw a rainbow on top of the Chuskai Mountains and they knew that the rainbow had picked up the children. So they had a little ceremony and made four footprints outside of their houses out of white corn, and four footprints and handprints of corn pollen inside the houses, and prayed. They sent a messenger to another village of Kih-ah-ah people and to all the other villages, that they must keep the days holy until these children came home again.

The people were right, for the rainbow had taken up the children and carried them to the Chuskai Mountains, and then west to the seashore. And on the rainbow stood Hashje-altye and Hashje-hogahn, one on each side of the children. When they reached the seashore, the children could see the Island across the sea and flowers were growing all along the beach very thickly. Estsan-ah-tlehay had made thirty-two trails from the shore to the Island going down under the sea in spiral shape. And Hashje-altye (the Talking God) asked the boy and girl which trail they would take to reach Estsan-ah-tlehay. They selected the right trail, and it led them under the sea to the house of Estsan-ah-tlehay, and Hashje-altye led the way.

When they reached the Island, they went under it to the great crystal house, and entered it, and there they saw an old, old woman lying on the floor. Hashje-altye said to her: "Here are your children." And the old woman asked if one was a boy and one was a girl, and they said: "Yes." Estsan-ah-tlehay tried to rise, but she was so old she could hardly move, so Hashje-altye helped her, and she crawled to the door and raised the bar that closed it, and went into the altar in the inner room. Then she appeared again stronger and younger, and then went in again to the altar. Four times she did this, and the last time she appeared she was only about sixteen years old and she danced about very happily. She summoned the spirits of the Yeh and told them to bring a bowl of white crystal for the children to bathe in. The female Yehs washed the girl, and the male Yehs washed the boy and they dressed the boy and girl in white shoes and clothing, and put feathers in their hair as is now done in the fire dance, and then they fed them. Estsan-ah-tlehay told the children that the reason why she had sent for them was that she wanted to give them prayer sticks and medicine called Siss-bayis-kothy, which is a belt of medicine, and she gave them these things and told them stories all night long. Next morning Estsan-ah-tlehay mounted to a peak on the Island with the children and drew the whole earth up to her. As she stood there, and as they looked towards the east, they saw many sheep; and at the south they saw all kinds of plants and rain watering the plants; and to the west they looked and saw all kinds of horses and mules and donkeys; and to the north they saw all kinds of game, deer, lions, and wild animals. And there is a song for everything they saw on the mountain. It is called Estsan-eh-beyin, which means "The Changing-Woman's Song." [9] In three days the children learned all the songs of the sheep, horses, corn and all other things. These songs mean to bring forth and multiply. After four days they had learned every-thing and Estsan-ah-tlehay said she would go part way back with them.

Then Estsan-ah-tlehay said to the children: "I want to learn your songs." But they knew only two, which they sang for her, one of which was called Ahchini-beyin. That night they held a Council and all the gods came and they spread a buckskin and a cotton robe for the children to sit on, and they put the medicine belt down on the robes by the children. The gods sang all night, and at daybreak, Estsan-ah-tlehay showed them many sheep, cows, and horses at Siss-nah-tyel (near Kim-betoh, New Mexico), and said to them: "I give these animals to you, and now you know my songs, and you must go back and teach them to your people and tell them never to forget them. I will give you your names. The boy will be called Nahtahyah-ni-zhehni, which means the Establishment-and-End-of-the-Created-Law or Standing-for-the-Law. The girl will be named Non-napah, which means White-Shell-Woman-of-the-Future. And these names must not be forgotten."

The two children went back in a flash on the rainbow to their home, Kebeh-eteen. As they approached it, Hashje-altye gave his call four times, and the people saw them coming all dressed in feathers. Hashje-altye sang to the people the last hogahn-beyin (House Song), and the children taught Estsan-ah-tlehay's song to the head men. Two men learned their song by heart and taught it to the other people. When all the ceremonies, Yeh-bechai, Bear Cerernony, and all, had been learned, Begochiddy left the people and never appeared again.

Begochiddy said: "Possibly some day this world will be destroyed by flood, fire or cyclone, and then I will come again. The Rainbow will give you the signs, and if the Rainbow lasts all day long, that will mean that something dreadful is going to happen. Two other bad signs are a Rainbow around the Sun, which means rain or sandstorm, and if Giss-dil-yessi does not grow."

[1] The Black God sandpainting of the Tleji or Yehbechai ceremony has to do with this part of the story.
[2] The sandpainting of the place of emergence has to do with this part of the story.
[3] Female and male respectively.
[4] This was the first mother-in-law trouble.
[5] Hasteen Klah noted that from this point present day Navajos know the story.
[6] Hasteen Klah said: "The only two people who know the Creation Song today are Nakai-John (Klah's older brother) and myself." Klah died in 1936.
[7] Klah stated that there are six of these feathers in existence.
[8] Natahnapah, a fire-dance priest of Nava, New Mexico, was of this clan.
[9] Hasteen Klah sang the Estsan-eh-beyin.

Navajo Ceremonial Songs

Based on the Creation Myth

The following songs, from the Museum's collection of over 1500 records, have been selected to show the connection between the songs used in Navajo ceremonials and the Creation Myth narrative.

These songs, sung by Hasteen Klah, were recorded and translated by Dr. Harry Hoijer and edited by Dr. George Herzog.

1. SONG OF THE ETHKAY-NAH-ASHI [1]

That which is good
    May it be made as offering to him
    May it be made as offering to him

The young man who walks in the darkness
    May it be made as offering to him
    May it be made as offering to him
The beautiful black bead
    May it be made as offering to him
    May it be made as offering to him
The beautiful sparkling stone
    May it be made as offering to him
    May it be made as offering to him
The beautiful blue pollen
    May it be made as offering to him
    May it be made as offering to him
The beautiful corn pollen
    May it be made as offering to him
    May it be made as offering to him
They will be exchanged tor his mind, his voice;
    May it be made as offering to him.

The young woman of the dusk
    May it be made as offering to her
    May it be made as offering to her
The beautiful white shell
    May it be made as offering to her
    May it be made as offering to her

The beautiful sparkling stone
    May it be made as offering to her
    May it be made as offering to her
The beautiful blue pollen
    May it be made as offering to her
    May it be made as offering to her
The beautiful corn pollen
    May it be made as offering to her
    May it be made as offering to her
They will be exchanged for her voice, her mind;
    May they be made as offering to her.

That which is good
    May it be made as offering to her
    May it be made as offering to her.

2. SONG OF THE FLOOD [2]

The first man—you are his child, he is your child
The first woman—you are her child, she is your child
The water monster—you are his child, he is your child
The black sea-horse—you are his child, he is your child
The black snake—you are his child, he is your child
The big blue snake—you are his child, he is your child
The white corn—you are his child, he is your child
The yellow corn—you are his child, he is your child
The corn pollen—you are his child, he is your child
The corn beetle—you are his child, he is your child
Sahanahray—you are his child, he is your child
Bekayhozhon—you are his child, he is your child

3. SECOND SONG OF THE FLOOD

They are running from the water, I came up with it
    When my spiritual power was strong, I came up with it
    When it was holy, I came up with it
They start moving from the water, I came up with it
    When my spiritual power was strong, I came up with it
    When it was holy, I came up with it
The rocks which extend upward, I came up with them
    When my spiritual power was strong, I came up with them
    When it was holy, I came up with them
The mountains which extend upward, I came up with them
    When my spiritual power was strong, I came up with them.

When it was holy, I came up with them
The waters which extend upward, I came up with them
　　When my spiritual power was strong, I came up with them
　　When it was holy, I came up with them
The clouds which extend upward, I came up with them
　　When my spiritual power was strong, I came up with them
　　When it was holy, I came up with them
The mists which extend upward, I came up with them
　　When my spiritual power was strong, I came up with them
　　When it was holy, I came up with them
They arrived at the sky, I came up with them
　　When my spiritual power was strong, I came up with them
　　When it was holy, I came up with them
They came through the sky, I came up with them
　　When my spiritual power was strong, I came up with them
　　When it was holy, I came up with them
They came up to it, I came up with them
　　When my spiritual power was strong, I came up with them
　　When it was holy, I came up with them
They are camping in it, I came up with them
　　When my spiritual power was strong, I came up with them
　　When it was holy, I came up with them
They are moving away from each other, I came up with them
　　When my spiritual power was strong, I came up with them
　　When it was holy, I came up with them.

4. SONG OF THE SUN AND MOON

The first man holds it in his hands
He holds the sun in his hands
In the center of the sky, he holds it in his hands
As he holds it in his hands, it starts upward.

The first woman holds it in her hands
She holds the moon in her hands
In the center of the sky, she holds it in her hands
As she holds it in her hands, it starts upward.

The first man holds it in his hands
He holds the sun in his hands
In the center of the sky, he holds it in his hands
As he holds it in his hands, it starts downward.

The first woman holds it in her hands

She holds the moon in her hands
In the center of the sky, she holds it in her hands
As she holds it in her hands, it starts downward.

5. SONG OF THE LADDER

The ladder, the ladder, the ladder, the ladder
The ladder, the ladder, the ladder, the ladder.

From down in the Emergence Pit—the ladder, the ladder
The Talking God moves with me up the black ladder—the ladder, the ladder
He moves with the rainbow—the ladder, the ladder
To the edge of the Emergence Pit—the ladder, the ladder;
Blue-bird is humming before me—the ladder, the ladder
Corn-beetle is humming behind me—the ladder, the ladder
I, I am Sahanahray Bekayhozhon—the ladder, the ladder
Before me all is beautiful—the ladder, the ladder
Behind me all is beautiful—the ladder, the ladder.

The ladder, the ladder, the ladder, the ladder.

From down in the Emergence Pit—the ladder, the ladder
The House God moves with me up the blue ladder—the ladder, the ladder
He moves with the lightning—the ladder, the ladder
To the edge of the Emergence Pit—the ladder, the ladder;
Corn-beetle is humming behind me—the ladder, the ladder
Blue-bird is humming before me—the ladder, the ladder
I, I am Sahanahray Bekayhozhon—the ladder, the ladder
Behind me all is beautiful—the ladder, the ladder
Before me all is beautiful—the ladder, the ladder.

The ladder, the ladder, the ladder, the ladder
The ladder, the ladder, the ladder, the ladder.

6. THERE ARE NO PEOPLE SONG

You say there were no people
        Smoke was spreading [3]
You say there were no people
        Smoke was spreading.

First Man was the very first to emerge, they say,
        Smoke was spreading
He brought with him the various robes and precious things they say,

Smoke was spreading
He brought with him the white corn and the yellow corn, they say,
    Smoke was spreading
He brought with him the various animals and the growing things, they say,
    Smoke was spreading.

You say there were no people
    Smoke was spreading.

First Woman was the very first to emerge, they say,
    Smoke was spreading
She brought with her the various precious things and robes, they say, [4]
    Smoke was spreading
She brought with her the yellow corn and the varicolored corn, they say,
    Smoke was spreading
She brought with her the various animals and the growing things, they say,
    Smoke was spreading.

You say there were no people
    Smoke was spreading
You say there were no people
    Smoke was spreading.

7. THE SONG OF COYOTE WHO STOLE THE FIRE

I am frivolous Coyote; I wander around
I have seen the Black God's fire; I wander around
I stole his fire from him; I wander around
I have it! I have it!

I am changing Coyote; I wander around
I have seen the bumble-bee's fire; I wander around
I stole his fire from him; I wander around
I have it! I have it!

8. SWEATHOUSE SONG

The earth has been laid down, the earth has been laid down
The earth has been laid down, it has been made.

The earth spirit has been laid down
It is covered over with the growing things, it has been laid down
Sahanahray Bekayhozhon have been laid down
The earth has been laid down, it has been made.

The sky has been set up, the sky has been set up
The sky has been set up, it has been made.

The black sky has been set up
It is covered over with the heavenly bodies, it has been set up
Sahanahray Bekayhozhon have been set up
The sky has been set up, it has been made.

The mountains have been laid down, the mountains have been laid down
The mountains have been laid down, they have been made.

The mountain spirits have been laid down
They are covered over with all the animals, they have been laid down
Sahanahray Bekayhozhon have been laid down
The mountains have been laid down, they have been made.

The waters have been laid down, the waters have been laid down
The waters have been laid down, they have been made.

The water spirits have been laid down
They are covered over with the water pollen, [5] they have been laid down
Sahanahray Bekayhozhon have been laid down
The waters have been laid down, they have been made.

The clouds have been set up, the clouds have been set up
The clouds have been set up, the clouds have been made.

The black clouds have been set up
They are covered over with the male rain, they have been set up
Sahanahray Bekayhozhon have been set up
The clouds have been set up, they have been made.

The fog has been set up, the fog has been set up
The fog has been set up, the fog has been made.

The black fog has been set up
It is covered over with female rain, it has been set up
Sahanahray Bekayhozhon have been set up
The fog has been set up, it has been made.

9. SECOND SWEATHOUSE SONG

There is no wood, there is no wood

There is no wood, there is no wood
    There is no wood.

Beaver man talks to me
He gives me his wood
With it I take a sweat bath
    There is no wood, there is no wood.
Sahanahray Bekayhozhon
They give me their wood
With it I take a sweat bath
    There is no wood, there is no wood.

There is no wood, there is no wood
There is no wood, there is no wood.

10. THIRD SWEATHOUSE SONG

There are no stones, there are no stones
There are no stones, there are no stones
    There are no stones.

Mountain sheep man talks to me
He gives me his stones
With them I take a sweat bath
    There are no stones, there are no stones.

Sahanahray Bekayhozhon
They give me their stones
With them I take a sweat bath
    There are no stones, there are no stones.

There are no stones, there are no stones
There are no stones, there are no stones.

11. FOURTH SWEATHOUSE SONG

There is no fire, there is no fire
There is no fire, there is no fire
    There is no fire.

Bumble-bee man talks to me.
He gives me his fire
With it I take a sweat bath
    There is no fire, there is no fire.

Sahanahray Bekayhozhon
They give me their fire
With it I take a sweat bath
    There is no fire, there is no fire.

There is no fire, there is no fire
There is no fire, there is no fire.

12. FIFTH SWEATHOUSE SONG

There is no water, there is no water
There is no water, there is no water
    There is no water.

Muskrat girl talks to me
She gives me her water
With it I take a sweat bath
    There is no water, there is no water.

Sahanahray Bekayhozhon
They give me their water
With it I take a sweat bath
    There is no water, there is no water.

There is no water, there is no water
There is no water, there is no water.

13. SIXTH SWEATHOUSE SONG

He made it, he made it, they say.

Right on the edge of the Place of Emergence, he made it
First Man, he made it
The little darkness, he made it [6]
Of the various robes, he made it
Sahanahray Bekayhozhon.

He made it, he made it, they say.

Right on the edge of the Place of Emergence, she made it
First Woman, she made it
The little daylight, she made it [7]
Of the various precious things, she made it

Sahanahray Bekayhozhon.

She made it, she made it, they say

14. HOUSE SONG (FROM THE HAIL CHANT)

Here the burning firewood
Here the burning firewood
Here the burning firewood
Here the burning firewood
Here the burning firewood

Below the East, the burning firewood
The fire of the trees is the burning firewood
The fire of Sahanahray is the burning firewood
The fire of Bekayhozhon is the burning firewood
Here all around it is warm, here the burning firewood
     The burning firewood.

Below the West, the burning firewood
The fire of the trees is the burning firewood
The fire of Sahanahray is the burning firewood
The fire of Bekayhozhon is the burning firewood
Here all around it is warm, here the burning firewood
     The burning firewood.

Below the South, the burning firewood
The fire of the trees is the burning firewood
The fire of Sahanahray is the burning firewood
The fire of Bekayhozhon is the burning firewood
Here all around it is warm, here the burning firewood
     The burning firewood.

Below the North, the burning firewood
The Big Star blazing is the burning firewood
The fire of Sahanahray is the burning firewood
The fire of Bekayhozhon is the burning firewood
Here all around it is warm, here the burning firewood
     The burning firewood

Here the burning firewood
Here the burning firewood
Here the burning firewood
Here the burning firewood
Here the burning firewood.

15. SONG OF CREATING PEOPLE (FROM THE HAIL CHANT)

Hozhoni, hozhoni, hozhoni
Hozhoni, hozhoni, hozhoni.
The Earth, its life am I, hozhoni, hozhoni
The Earth, its feet are my feet, hozhoni, hozhoni
The Earth, its legs are my legs, hozhoni, hozhoni
The Earth, its body is my body, hozhoni, hozhoni
The Earth, its thoughts are my thoughts, hozhoni, hozhoni
The Earth, its speech is my speech, hozhoni, hozhoni
The Earth, its down-feathers are my down-feathers, hozhoni, hozhoni.

The sky, its life am I, hozhoni, hozhoni— [8]
The mountains, their life am I—
Rain-mountain, its life am I—
Changing-Woman, her life am I—
The Sun, its life am I—
Talking God, his life am I—
House God, his life am I—
White corn, its life am I—
Yellow corn, its life am I—
Corn-pollen, its life am I—
The corn-beetle, its life am I—

Hozhoni, hozhoni, hozhoni
Hozhoni, hozhoni, hozhoni.

16. MOUNTAIN SONG

He can see everywhere, he can see everywhere, he can see everywhere
    He can see everywhere.

From below the East, he can see everywhere
From the top of Pelado Peak, he can see everywhere
From the top of the White Shell Mountain, he can see everywhere
From the top of the Talking Mountain, he can see everywhere
From the top of Sahanahray Bekayhozhon, he can see everywhere
The Talking God Boy, he can see everywhere
Through twelve pieces of obsidian, he can see everywhere.

He can see everywhere, he can see everywhere, he can see everywhere
    He can see everywhere.

From below the West, he can see everywhere

From the top of San Francisco Peak, he can see everywhere
From the top of the Abalone Mountain, he can see everywhere
From the top of the Talking Mountain, he can see everywhere
From the top of Sahanahray Bekayhozhon, he can see everywhere
The House God Boy, he can see everywhere
Through twelve pieces of obsidian, he can see everywhere.

He can see everywhere, he can see everywhere, he can see everywhere
    He can see everywhere.

From below the South, he can see everywhere
From the top of Mount Taylor, he can see everywhere
From the top of the Turquoise Mountain, he can see everywhere
From the top of the Talking Mountain, he can see everywhere
From the top of Sahanahray Bekayhozhon, he can see everywhere
The Male God Boy, he can see everywhere
Through twelve pieces of obsidian, he can see everywhere.

He can see everywhere, he can see everywhere, he can see everywhere
    He can see everywhere.

From below the North, she can see everywhere
From the top of San Juan Mountain, she can see everywhere
From the top of the Jet Mountain, she can see everywhere
From the top of the Talking Mountain, she can see everywhere
From the top of Sahanahray Bekayhozhon, she can see everywhere
The Female God Girl, she can see everywhere
Through twelve pieces of obsidian, she can see everywhere.

She can see everywhere, she can see everywhere, she can see everywhere
    She can see everywhere.

17. SONG OF HOW THE SUN WAS MADE

They emerged; they say he is planning it [9]
They emerged; they say he is planning it
They emerged; they say he is planning it.

Right on the edge of the Emergence Pit, they say he is planning it
In the center of First Man's hogahn, they say he is planning it
In the center of a hogahn of robes, they say he is planning it
On top of a pile of robes, they say he is planning it
The sun will be created, they say he is planning it
His face will be blue, they say he is planning it

His eyes will be black, they say he is planning it
His chin will be yellow, they say he is planning it
His horns will be blue, they say he is planning it
Black is around him, they say he is planning it
White is around him, they say he is planning it
Yellow is around him, they say he is planning it
Red is around him, they say he is planning it
In his body there is danger, they say he is planning it
Sahanahray Bekayhozhon it shall be, they say he is planning it.

They emerged; they say he is planning it
They emerged; they say he is planning it
They emerged; they say he is planning it.

Right on the edge of the Emergence Pit, they say he is planning it
In the center of the First Woman's hogahn, they say he is planning it
In the center of a hogahn of precious things, they say he is planning it
On top of a pile of precious things, they say he is planning it
The moon will be created, they say he is planning it
His face will be white, they say he is planning it
His eyes will be black, they say he is planning it
His chin will be yellow, they say he is planning it
His horns will be white, they say he is planning it
Black is around him, they say he is planning it
Yellow is around him, they say he is planning it
Blue is around him, they say he is planning it
Red is around him, they say he is planning it
In his body there is danger, they say he is planning it
Sahanahray Bekayhozhon it shall be, they say he is planning it.

They emerged; they say he is planning it
They emerged; they say he is planning it
They emerged; they say he is planning it. [10]

18. SONG OF SUN AND MOON

From far away he commands; he rises, see him!
From far away he commands; he rises, see him!
From far away he commands; he rises, see him!

From far below the East he commands; he rises, see him!
The Sun commands; he rises, see him!
His face is blue; see him!
His eye-sockets are black; see him!

His chin is yellow; see him!
His horns are blue; see him!
Around him is black; see him!
Around him is white; see him!
Around him is yellow; see him!
Around him is red; see him!
In his body is danger; see him!
A round corn (kernel) moves through the air; [11] see him!
See how he shines over all the earth; see him!
See how he shines over all the earth to where earth and sky meet; see him!
See how he shines over all the earth to where mountain and sky meet; see him!
See how he shines over all the earth to where water and sky meet; see him!
See how he shines over all the earth to where the growing things and the sky meet; see him!
See how he shines over all the earth to the horizon of the heavenly bodies; see him!
Sahanahray Bekayhozhon; see him!

From far away he commands; he rises, see him!
From far away he commands; he rises, see him!
From far away he commands; he rises, see him!
From below the East he commands; he rises, see him!
The Moon commands; he rises, see him!
His face is white; see him!
His eye-sockets are black; see him!
His chin is yellow; see him!
His horns are white; see him!
Around him it is black; see him!
Around him it is yellow; see him!
Around him it is blue; see him!
Around him it is red; see him!
In his body is danger; see him!
A round corn (kernel) moves through the air; see him!
See how he shines over all the earth; see him!
See how he shines over all the earth to where earth and sky meet; see him!
See how he shines over all the earth to where mountain and sky meet; see him!
See how he shines over all the earth to where water and sky meet; see him!
See how he shines over all the earth to where the growing things and the sky meet; see him!
See how he shines over all the earth to the horizon of the heavenly bodies; see him!
Sahanahray Bekayhozhon; see him!

From far away he commands; he rises, see him!
From far away he commands; he rises, see him!
From far away he commands; he rises, see him!

19. WHERE THE STARS WERE MADE

Man will be created, man will be created.

The first man, the first woman
> From them, man will be created, man will be created
Sahanahray Bekayhozhon
> From them, man will be created, man will be created
The Big Dipper, the Little Dipper
> From them, man will be created, man will be created
Sahanahray Bekayhozhon
> From them, man will be created, man will be created
The Pleiades, the first constellation (1)
> From them, man will be created, man will be created
Sahanahray Bekayhozhon
> From them, man will be created, man will be created
The second constellation, (2) the third constellation (3)
> From them, man will be created, man will be created
Sahanahray Bekayhozhon
> From them, man will be created, man will be created
The "Rabbit's Tracks" (4), the Milky Way
> From them, man will be created, man will be created
Sahanahray Bekayhozhon
> From them, man will be created, man will be created
Pelado Peak, Mount Taylor
> From them, man will be created, man will be created
Sahanahray Bekayhozhon
> From them, man will be created, man will be created
San Francisco Peak, San Juan Mountain
> From them, man will be created, man will be created
The Talking God, the House God
> From them, man will be created, man will be created
Sahanahray Bekayhozhon
> From them, man will be created, man will be created
The white corn, the yellow corn
> From them, man will be created, man will be created
Sahanahray Bekayhozhon
> From them, man will be created, man will be created
The corn-pollen, the corn-beetle

From them, man will be created, man will be created
Sahanahray Bekayhozhon
From them, man will be created, man will be created

Man will be created, man will be created. [12]

20. WHEN THEY SAW EACH OTHER

The Earth is looking at me; she is looking up at me
I am looking down on her
I am happy, she is looking at me
I am happy, I am looking at her.

The Sun is looking at me; he is looking down on me
I am looking up at him
I am happy, he is looking at me
I am happy, I am looking at him.

The Black Sky is looking at me; he is looking down on me
I am looking up at him
I am happy, he is looking at me
I am happy, I am looking at him.

The Moon is looking at me; he is looking down on me
I am looking up at him.
I am happy, he is looking at me.
I am happy, I am looking at him.

The North is looking at me; he is looking across at me
I am looking across at him
I am happy, he is looking at me
I am happy, I am looking at him.

21. CRADLE SONG

Hush, hush, hush, hush
Hush, hush, hush, hush! [13]

On the edge of the place of Emergence, hush!
On top of the Johleen Mountain, hush!
White-Shell-Woman is here, hush!
The Talking God is here, hush!
The white corn, hush!
About its feet—hush—the earth; hush!

At the end of its leaves—hush—the black cloud; hush!
At its water—hush—the male rain; hush!
Its big stalk—hush—my body; hush!
Placed on alternate sides—hush—its pollen; hush!
On its flowers—hush—its pollen; hush!
On its hair—hush—the rainbow; hush!
On its kernels—hush—the white shell; hush!
Before it—hush—the Talking God; hush!
Behind it—hush—the House God; hush!
Under it—hush—the lizard; hush!
Above it—hush—the night bird; hush!
On top of it—hush—the blue bird; hush!
All around it—hush—the corn beetle; hush!
Under it—hush—the earth; hush!
Above it—hush—the black sky; hush!
Sahanahray Bekayhozhon, hush!
Before it all is beautiful, hush!
Behind it all is beautiful, hush!

Hush, hush, hush, hush
Hush, hush, hush, hush!

On the edge of the place of Emergence, hush!
On top of Huerfano Mountain, hush!
Changing-Woman is here, hush!
The House God is here, hush!
The yellow corn, hush!
About its feet—hush—the earth; hush!
At the end of its leaves—hush—the black fog; hush!
At its waters—hush—the female rain; hush!
Its big stalk—hush—my body; hush!
Placed on alternate sides—hush—its pollen; hush!
On its flowers—hush—the pollen; hush!
On its hair—hush—the rainbow; hush!
On its kernels—hush—the abalone; hush!
Behind it—hush—the House God; hush!
Before it—hush—the Talking God; hush!
Above it—hush—the night bird; hush!
Under it—hush—the lizard; hush!
On top of it—hush—the corn-beetle; hush!
All around it—hush—the growing things; hush!
Above it—hush—the black sky; hush!
Under it—hush—the earth; hush!
Sahanahray Bekayhozhon, hush!

Behind it all is beautiful, hush!
Before it all is beautiful, hush!

Hush, hush, hush, hush
Hush, hush, hush, hush!

22. SONG OF THE FIRST PUBERTY CEREMONY

She moves, she moves
She moves, she moves.

White-Shell-Woman, she moves
Her shoes of white shell, she moves
Her shoes trimmed in black, she moves
Her shoe-strings of white shell, she moves
Her leggings of white shell, she moves
Her garters of white shell, she moves
Her buckskin-fringed trousers of white shell, she moves
Her dancing-skirt of white shell, she moves
Her belt of white shell, she moves
Her shirt of white shell, she moves
Her bracelet of white shell, she moves
Her necklace of white shell, she moves
Her earrings of white shell, she moves
The pollen of the various robes is placed in her mouth, she moves
Her visor of white shell, she moves
A white shell has been placed on her forehead, she moves
Her feather of white shell, she moves
Above her a male blue-bird dances about beautifully, she moves
He sings: his voice is beautiful, she moves
Sahanahray Bekayhozhon, she moves
Before her all is beautiful, she moves
Behind her all is beautiful, she moves.

She moves, she moves
She moves, she moves.

23. SECOND SONG OF THE PUBERTY CEREMONY [14]

She moves, she moves
She moves, she moves.

Changing-Woman, she moves
Her shoes of turquoise, she moves

Her shoes of turquoise trimmed in black, she moves
Her shoe-strings of turquoise, she moves
Her leggings of turquoise, she moves
Her garters of turquoise, she moves
Her buckskin-fringed trousers of turquoise, she moves
Her dancing-skirt of turquoise, she moves
Her belt of turquoise, she moves
Her shirt of turquoise, she moves
Her bracelet of turquoise, she moves
Her necklace of turquoise, she moves
Her earrings of turquoise, she moves
The pollen of the various precious things has been placed in
her mouth, she moves
Her visor of turquoise, she moves
A turquoise has been placed on her forehead, she moves
Her feather of turquoise, she moves
Above her a female blue-bird dances about beautifully, she moves
She sings: her voice is beautiful, she moves
Sahanahray Bekayhozhon, she moves
Behind her all is beautiful, she moves
Before her all is beautiful, she moves.

She moves, she moves
She moves, she moves.

24. THE OLD AGE SPIRITS [15]

From far away they are coming
From far away they are coming, from far away they are coming
From far away they are coming
From far away they are coming.

I am the child of Changing-Woman; they are coming
From the road below the East; they are coming,

Old age is coming for them; they are coming, from far away they are coming
From far away they are coming
From far away they are coming.

I am the grandson of Changing-Woman; they are coming
On the many roads below the East; they are coming,

Old age is coming for them; they are coming, from far away they are coming
From far away they are coming
From far away they are coming.

25. SONG OF OLD AGE (FROM THE BLESSING CHANT) [16]

Age, age
It goes about above, age, age.

It goes about above the Earth, age, they say
It goes about beneath, beneath Sahanahray Bekayhozhon, age, they say
It goes about beneath, age, they say
It goes about beneath, age, they say.

It goes about beneath, below the Sky, age, they say
It goes about beneath, beneath Sahanahray Bekayhozhon, age, they say
It goes about beneath, age, they say
It goes about beneath, age, they say.

Above all the mountains, age, they say
It goes about beneath, beneath Sahanahray Bekayhozhon, age, they say
It goes about beneath, age, they say
It goes about beneath, age, they say.

It goes about beneath the Sun, age, they say
It goes around it, around Sahanahray Bekayhozhon, age, they say
It goes about beneath, age, they say
It goes about beneath, age, they say.

It goes about around them, all the springs, age, they say
It goes about around them, around Sahanahray Bekayhozhon, age, they say
It goes about around them, age, they say
It goes about around them, age, they say.

It goes about around them.

26. SONG OF THE RAINBOW [17]

It has been stretched over me, it has been stretched over me
It has been stretched over me, it has been stretched over me
It has been stretched over me, it has been stretched over me
It has been stretched over me, it has been stretched over me.

I am the Talking God; it has been stretched over me
Seven rainbows appear; it has been stretched over me
Seven kinds of robes appear; it has been stretched over me
Seven kinds of precious things appear; it has been stretched over me
I am Sahanahray Bekayhozhon; it has been stretched over me.

It has been stretched over me, it has been stretched over me
It has been stretched over me, it has been stretched over me
It has been stretched over me, it has been stretched over me
It has been stretched over me, it has been stretched over me.

I am the House God; it has been stretched over me
Five strings of beads appear; it has been stretched over me
Five kinds of precious things appear; it has been stretched over me
Five kinds of robes appear; it has been stretched over me
I am Sahanahray Bekayhozhon; it has been stretched over me.

It has been stretched over me, it has been stretched over me
It has been stretched over me, it has been stretched over me
It has been stretched over me, it has been stretched over me
It has been stretched over me, it has been stretched over me.

27. SONG OF THE WHITE SHELL PRAYER-STICKS

Beautiful—I wander about
Beautiful—I wander about
Beautiful—I wander about.

I am the House God, I wander about,
    I—beautiful—wander about
Where the (logs) of my house lie toward each other, I wander about,
    I—beautiful—wander about
At the far wall of my house, I wander about,
    I—beautiful—wander about
In the center of my house, I wander about,
    I—beautiful—wander about
In the fireplace of my house, I wander about,
    I—beautiful—wander about
In the inside door-corner of my house, I wander about,
    I—beautiful—wander about
In the entrance-way of my house, I wander about,
    I—beautiful—wander about
The Talking Gods are standing all around my house, I wander about,
    I—beautiful—wander about
The House Gods are standing all around my house, I wander about,
    I—beautiful—wander about
The white corn boys are standing all around my house, I wander about,
    I—beautiful—wander about
The yellow corn girls are standing all around my house, I wander about,

I—beautiful—wander about
The corn-pollen boys are standing all around my house, I wander about,
    I—beautiful—wander about
The corn-beetle girls are standing all around my house, I wander about,
    I—beautiful—wander about
The sky surrounds all of my house, I wander about,
    I—beautiful—wander about
Sahanahray Bekayhozhon surround all of my house, I wander about,
    I—beautiful—wander about

Before me it is beautiful, I wander about,
    I—beautiful—wander about
Behind me it is beautiful, I wander about,
    I—beautiful—wander about
Below me it is beautiful, I wander about,
    I—beautiful—wander about
Above me it is beautiful, I wander about,
    I—beautiful—wander about
All around me it is beautiful, I wander about,
    I—beautiful—wander about.

Beautiful—I wander about
Beautiful—I wander about
Beautiful—I wander about.

28. SONG OF THE CHIEF'S HOGAHN [18]

He is thinking about it, he is thinking about it
He is thinking about it, he is thinking about it.

The main beams of the earth will be main beams; he is thinking about it
The main beams of the wood spirit will be main beams; he is thinking about it
The main beams of Sahanahray Bekayhozhon will be main beams; he is thinking about it.

The main beams of the mountain spirit will be main beams; he is thinking about it
The main beams of the wood spirit will be main beams; he is thinking about it
The main beams of Sahanahray Bekayhozhon will be main beams; he is thinking about it.

The main beams of the water spirit will be main beams; he is thinking about

it
The main bearns of the wood spirit will be main beams; he is thinking about it
The main beams of Sahanahray Bekayhozhon will be main beams; he is thinking about it.

The main beams of the corn spirit will be main beams; he is thinking about it
The main bearns of the wood spirit will be main beams; he is thinking about it
The main beams of Sahanahray Bekayhozhon will be main beams; he is thinking about it.

He is thinking about it, he is thinking about it
He is thinking about it, he is thinking about it.

29. SONG OF THE TWO CHILDREN (FROM THE HAIL CHANT)

Come, come! Come, come!
Come, come! Come, come!

I am the child of White-Shell-Woman—come! Come, come!
Rainbow makes a wavy trail over it—come! Come, come!
On top of Mount Pedernal—come! Come, come!
Where White-Shell-Woman was born—come! Come, come!
Tracks of corn-pollen on top—come! Come, come!
Where White-Shell-Woman arrived—come! Come, come!
I arrived there too—come! Come, come!
Around me black cloud, it surrounds me—come! Come, come!
Around me male rain, it surrounds me—come! Come, come!
Around me all plants, beautiful all around me—come! Come, come.
Around me corn-pollen, beautiful all around me—come! Come, come!
Sahanahray Bekayhozhon, where they were born—come! Come, come!
I am the child of Sahanahray Bekayhozhon—come! Come, come!
Before me is peace—come! Come, come!
Behind me is peace-come! Come, come!

Come, come! Come, come!

I am the child of Changing-Woman—come! Come, come!
Sunbeams make a wavy trail over it—come! Come, come!
On top of Huerfano Mountain—come! Come, come!
Where Changing-Woman was born—come! Come, come!
Tracks of corn-pollen on top—come! Come, Come!
Where Changing-Woman arrived—come! Come, come!

I arrive there too—come! Come, come!
Around me black fog, it surrounds me—come! Come, come!
Around me female rain, it surrounds me—come! Come, come!
Around me blue-birds are singing, all around me—come! Come, come!
Around me corn-beetles are humming, all around me—come! Come, come!
Where Sahanahray Bekayhozhon were born—come! Come, come!
I am the child of Sahanahray Bekayhozhon—come! Come, come!
Behind me is peace—come! Come, come!
Before me is peace—come! Come, come!

Come, come! Come, come!

30. SONG OF THE EARTH (FROM THE BLESSING CHANT)

The Earth is beautiful
The Earth is beautiful
The Earth is beautiful.

Below the East, the Earth, its face toward East,
    the top of its head is beautiful
The soles of its feet, they are beautiful
Its feet, they are beautiful
Its legs, they are beautiful
Its body, it is beautiful
Its chest, it is beautiful
Its breast, it is beautiful
Its head-feather, it is beautiful
The Earth is beautiful.
Below the West, the Sky, it is beautiful, its face toward West,
    the top of its head is beautiful— [19]
Below the East, the dawn, its face toward East,
    the top of its head is beautiful—
Below the West, the afterglow of sundown, its face toward West,
    the top of its head is beautiful—
Below the East, White Corn, its face toward East,
    the top of its head is beautiful—
Below the South, Blue Corn, its face toward South,
    the top of its head is beautiful—
Below the West, Yellow Corn, its face toward West,
    the top of its head is beautiful—
Below the North, Varicolored Corn, its face toward North,
    the top of its head is beautiful—
Below the East, Sahanahray, its face toward East,
    the top of its head is beautiful—

Below the West, Bekayhozhon, its face toward West,
 the top of its head is beautiful—
Below the East, corn-pollen, its face toward East,
 the top of its head is beautiful—
Below the West, the corn-beetle, its face toward West,
 the top of its head is beautiful—
The Earth is beautiful.

[1] The Ethkay-nah-ashi, literally "The two who go about together," are mentioned in the Creation story. The offerings are meant to be given to "The young man who walks in the darkness" and "The young woman of the dusk." This is the very first song of the Creation story as given by the singer Klah. Five songs with the same melody and text follow except that the refrain—May it be made as offering to him—is changed to:

 They have started off with it (the offering).

 They have taken (the offerings) away (for the dead).

 They have set (the offerings) down (for the dead).

 He picks (the offerings) up.

 He is pleased (with the offering).

Sandpainting No. 4, Series I, shows the Ethkay-nah-ashi.

[2] The Flood is expressed in Navajo by the phrase, "we are running from the waters." The Navajo words in the last two lines are esoteric expressions which are used only in songs and prarers. Their meaning is sacred and medicine-men disagree on their exact interpretation. The second word contains the Navajo word for "holy."

[3] Over the earth.

[4] "The various robes" include skins and possessions of soft materials which the Navajo contrast with "hard" possessions such as jewelry, translated with "precious things" here. Two songs with the same melody and text follow.

The first changes the refrain—*Smoke was spreading (over the earth)*—to: *Smoke streamed out (from behind them).* The second changes the refrain to: *He (First Man) commanded them, they heard them,* except the last line of each stanza where it has instead: *He on the chief mountain commanded them, they heard him.*

[5] "Water pollen" refers to the detritus carried by a stream and deposited in black streaks along the sides of the banks.

[6] "The little darkness" is a poetic reference to the sweathouse; "the little daylight" to the entrance of the sweathouse.

[7] 1. After each of the following first lines, the last six lines of the first stanza are repeated, substituting "Sky, mountains," etc. for "Earth."

The word *hozhoni* (meaning peace or beauty) indicates the perfect rhythm betwern man and the universe.—M. C. W.

[8] That is, the creator is planning the creation of the sun.

[9] Three songs with the same melody and text follow, except that they substitute for the refrain: *They say he is planning it,* the following: *They say he is talking about it; They say he has made it.*

[10] A poetic reference to the sun or moon.

(1) A constellation said to be near the Pleiades; literally: "The first one which is narrow."

(2) Unidentified, literally: "The old man with his legs apart."

(3) Unidentified, literally: "The cane of the first big one."

(4) Another constellation.

[11] A song with the same melody and text follows, except that the refrain: *Man will be created* is replaced by: *Man has increased (in numbers)*.

[12] The Navajo word translated here as "hush" is an interjection used by mothers to quiet crying babies.

[13] Two songs with the same melody and text follow, except that they substitute "abalone" and "jet" for "white shell" and "turquoise." Then come five groups of four songs each, substituting for the refrain "She moves": *She stands up, She stands, She dances, She jingles,* and: *(Her ornaments) crowd up on her again and again.* In all other details, they are identical with the first group of four songs.

[14] This song is about the journey of the two War-Gods to their father, the Sun, as referred to in the story. The odd divisions of the poem attempt to follow the musical treatment in the song, according to which the second and third repetition of the refrain-formula are joined together in the introduction. What would be the third line of the brief stanzas is joined to the refrain-sections that form the connective and the coda. Two songs with the same melody and text follow, except that they change *they are coming* in the refrain to: *They two are coming,* and: *Several of them are coming.*

[15] The singer commented: "On top of the Earth, below the Sky, below the Sun, among the small waters, old age goes around."

[16] Three songs with the same melody and text follow, substituting for the refrain: *He places it around me, It is beautiful on me,* and: *I have passed through it* (i.e., the ring formed by the rainbow).

[17] Three songs with the identical melody and text follow, except that they substitute for the refrain, *He is thinking about it; He is talking to them about it, They are placing them* (i.e., the main beams of the hogahn), and: *They laid them down.* Also, in the last song the phrase "will be main beams" is everywhere replaced by: "they are placing them".

[18] This song is sung by Changing-Woman when her two children visit her on her island, as recounted in the story. The singer stated that the song was sung when the patient steps into the footstep marks on the sandpainting, before he is made to sit down on it.

[19] The second to the ninth lines of the stanza are repeated to make a full stanza after each of the following introductory lines.

Hozhonji—Blessing Chant

I

The myth material of the Hozhonji is from the Navajo Creation Myth, or Story of the Emergence. This is the foundation of the Navajo religion and the explanation of the world as they know it. As told by Hasteen Klah in the preceding pages, the story starts in a dark world in which are the Great God, Begochiddy; the Fire God, Hashjeshjin; Salt Woman, Asheen Assun; Coyote, Mah-ih; and First Man and First Woman, the prototypes of Man on this earth. These pass upwards to the second blue world, and there Begochiddy begins by creating twins, male and female. Hashjeshjin, the Fire God, destroys them and out of their dead substance Begochiddy creates the Ethkay-nah-ashi (literally the two-who-go-together), and then, when he wishes to bring life to the rest of creation, breathes his spirit into the Ethkay-nah-ashi, and through them the newly created stars, nature, animals and finally Man, as he exists now, come to life. I include below some information on the mysterious Ethkay-nah-ashi, portrayed in the final sandpainting (Set I), as they are evidently basically connected with the Hozhonji ceremony and once apparently had a rite or ceremony of their own. This mystery of life coming through dead substance from God to Creation I have mentioned in my general introduction.

Later, the myth tells how, after beginning creation, these first Powers passed up to the third or yellow world where the first sin occurred, and then up to this world, which is the white world. In the ceremony as given by Hasteen Klah, the path upward is shown in the sandpaintings (Set I) with the colors of the four worlds along the path. The Hozhonji is the most universally understandable of all Navajo ceremonies, as it concerns the blessing of the path of Man, or of life itself, and all who are present at the final ceremony, whether initiate or not, are expected to walk along the path upward on the sandpainting. The first three sandpaintings illustrated are not used now, for the ceremony has become shortened so that it consists of an evening of singing and ceremonial bathing, the making of the sandpainting in the morning of the next day and singing all that night.

The ceremony used to be at least four days long because the first sandpainting in this series was made at quite a distance outside and east of the ceremonial Hogahn, and the first rite took place there. On the second day the second sandpainting was made nearer the Hogahn and east of it, and on the third day the third sandpainting was made outside the door of the Hogahn, and then the fourth sandpainting was made in the Hogahn and west of the fire as it is today.

Nowadays the ceremony is of one night and one day, and it has several unusual features. It begins in the evening with blessing the Hogahn by putting pollen up on the roof beams at the four directions, and singing. Next day the sandpainting is made not, as usual, out of rock sand, but of pollen and powdered plant substances. The person for whom the ceremony is given sits south of it and sings, holding what I believe to be the symbol of Estsan-ah-tlehay, the Changing Woman, who never appears in any sandpainting, though she is very holy. This symbolic object is an ear of corn, wreathed in strings of turquoise, white shell and other beads; and Klah, the Medicine Man, held another similar ear of corn. They also held pieces of so-called mirage stone, Hadahonigay, which look like striped stalactite, and a pair of small images made of this stone with inlaid features of turquoise. Tied together with prayer plumes, these images are probably a male and female symbol of the Ethkay-nah-ashi. After many songs had been sung, the person for whom the ceremony was being given, instead of being placed on the sandpainting for treatment as in all other ceremonies, walked in the footsteps on the painting up the path of life, following the Medicine Man. After them, walking in the footsteps, passed all the men, women, and children in the Hogahn, the women carrying the seed corn. Then the painting was covered with a blanket, and the patient, his family and Klah sat on it, facing east, and sang. The painting was left there, covered with the blanket, so the painting permanently blessed the Hogahn, becoming part of the earth floor.

These Hozhonji sand paintings are a form of prayer showing in a set of symbols the Navajos' aspiration towards higher things, and the last sandpainting, if understood, puts down the miracle of birth in a wonderfully spiritual way. They are nearer to the idea expressed in the Mandalas of Tibet than any of the other sandpaintings. Nearly all Medicine Men know the Hozhonji ceremony, but most of them give it without sandpaintings. Klah told me that one form of the Blessing Chant used to be held to bless the tame animals and some of the sandpaintings were made in the corral and along the path leading to it.

The medicine articles of the Hozhonji are always kept by the Medicine Man's family after he dies, for even if they are not used they bring blessing to those possessing them.

I include here all the information I have been able to gather about the Ethkay-nah-ashi and the ceremony connected with them. It is only the older priests and those really initiated who know about them. Most would call the figures in the last Hozhonji sandpainting (of set I) Nayenezgani and Tobachischin, but the ones who know the inner meaning say that the Ethkay-nah-ashi are in every ceremony, although exact knowledge of them has been lost. Even the Hopis and the people of Taos have heard of them.

Information from Hasteen Klah. The ceremony of the Ethkay-nah-ashi used to be given on the afternoon of the fourth sandpainting of the Yehbechai. Klah knew the prayers but did not have the medicine which always descended through a woman from the last expert who lived about 300 years ago. The medicine went to the priest at that time and then to his daughter who married west of the Chuskai Mountains.

The ceremony took place outside the Hogahn. The priest held the Ethkay-nah-ashi masks, and a man and the Yeh came up to him and danced toward the Ethkay-nah-ashi from the east, south, west and north. The man held a basket full of jewelry. The priest put the mask of the Ethkay-nah-ashi on the man's face and led him into the Hogahn. The Ethkay-nah-ashi belong to Begochiddy, the Great God, and are next in order to him in holiness. The earthly forms are small twins who ride on little deer which bear twin male deer, and these, when they have been smothered by pollen (killed without the shedding of blood) are made into Yehbechai masks.

In 1930, A. J. Newcomb and Klah went to see if they could find some masks of the Ethkay-nah-ashi which Father Berard Haile knew of, and they found them in the possession of a woman near Ganado who said they must never pass into the hands of a man when not in use. As far as Klah knew, there were two masks at Lukachukai and two near Houk.

Another form of the Ethkay-nah-ashi ceremony given many years ago near Crown Point was described by Klah as follows:

They made two paths of white cornmeal, radiating from the Hogahn in all four directions. There were two people who came from the east wearing Yehbechai masks, and the patient and the Medicine Man came out of the Hogahn wearing the masks of the Ethkay-nah-ashi, and they stood at the meeting of the paths of white meal, the Medicine Man standing at the north of the patient.

Klah thought this ceremony was given only in the Nan-tizi-hatral-nantso, which was like the ceremony of Kin-be-hatral with the screen of reeds, and the birds hanging over it, only, instead of the snakes' heads projecting from the screen there were Yehs (gods) in the holes of the Kin (screen). Behind the Kin there were two Yehs sitting facing each other who were grinding the medicine, while at the north a man with pumpkin shells tied all over him ground the incense.

At sundown, there was a dance of six dancers, the Kin-nakai like the Yehbechai, but painted differently. On the last day of the ceremony at noon six groups danced. From the east the Ih-ahe-tso, a woman and a man, arm in arm, the woman carrying a basket of beans, and these dancers came from the south, west, and north and then went away. The Kin-nakai dancers came next dancing at sundown. Afterward, the Willa-chee (red ant) dancers, all painted red with white hands. After these the Yah-da-del-trahe lifting their feet high. Then the Yeh-nant-eh in line, facing the Hogahn. Then Hashje-hogahn, then four Atsathle dancers like the first dance of the Yehbechai, then the Atsathle-etsosi, which are the usual dancers of the last night of the Yehbechai as it is done now.

Information from Estsan Hatrali Begay, son of the Woman Singer of Red Rock who gave the Kin-behatral and Tsilthkehji Nahtohe Ceremonies in 1937. He gives the Hozhonji - Blessing Chant, but uses no sandpaintings and no Kehtahns, and it is a prayer cerernony of only one day. The Ethkay-nah-ashi belong to the Blessing Chant and they are in all ceremonies. One of them comes from the morning light and one from the evening light. The relatives of Akdilthly, who live near Lukachukai, have two masks, one white, one blue. When these masks were investigated by Clyde Beyal and Mrs. Newcomb, the man who directed them to the woman who had the masks said no one dared to use them now because the last people who tried to use them all died. The masks were to be used to make someone who hated you friendly again, but when not used right the masks were so powerful that they killed those who used them. There was no sandpainting or ceremony used with them. The last person who used these masks was Hatrali Nahkloi. (Hasteen Nahkloi was Klah's teacher and gave Washington Matthews his version of the Yehbechai.)

The old woman who holds the masks now belongs to the Kih-ahni Clan. She had them in a roll of white cloth about fourteen inches long by eight inches in thickness. There were three inside wrappings; the first inside one must be white buckskin tied with buckskin thongs. When this was opened there were two other buckskin wrapped bundles. She sprinkled the whole thing with pollen, and then opened the two. Inside were two very beautiful Yeh masks made of the whitest buckskin, with blue faces. One was square and one round, each one surrounded with red hair which lobked like lamb or mountain sheep wool dyed red. The design on the faces was not visible because across each face lay four prayer-plume bundles. Mrs. Newcomb thought it was a very old Yehbechai medicine. This old woman said the bundles will go to her son if he ever learns to sing Yehbechai. There is another pair of masks owned by the family of a man called Denay-Nez-Begay who lived at Na-ah-tee.

Evidently a man can use the masks and medicine, but they must be kept in the hands of a woman when not in use.

II

The following description is of the Hozhonji ceremony as given by Bitahni-bedugai, an old Medicine Man who lived near Tohatchi. He died in 1939. Bitahni said that he was the third member of his family who had given this Blessing Chant. It came from Hasteen Tseh-nah-jinni, who was the uncle of Bitahni-bedugai, and lived at Andilth Chilthly. The sandpaintings mentioned are reproduced in Set II.

Early in the morning of the first day, the patient takes the medicine bundle in his hands and prays to Hashje-altye. Then a ceremonial bath is given him and he is wiped off with white meal, and puts on new clothes. His hair is untied. Then the first sandpainting of Hahjeenah, the Emergence, is made, and the patient holds pollen in his hands. The patient goes outside and ties up his hair, then comes in and sits at west of painting facing east, holding the medicine bundle, and prays. Afterwards he goes out of the Hogahn for the rest of the day.

In the evening the sandpainting of four mountains is made, with path and footsteps on it leading into the sandpainting. The patient enters, walking on the footsteps, and after him everyone in the Hogahn, with the Medicine Man coming last and rubbing out the path behind him. The patient sits on white circle in center and the Medicine Man on yellow circle and they pray. Then the Medicine Man puts both circles together and his patient sits on both and they sing and pray all night. The person sitting next to the door at the south takes pollen and touches his mouth and head with it, and all those in the Hogahn in turn do the same. Twelve very holy Hogahn songs are sung, as well as many others. Just before dawn twelve more very holy early morning songs are sung. The sandpainting is piled together and the patient sleeps on it for four nights, then he carries it out and puts it in the desert. After the Medicine Man gets home he sings twelve finishing songs to guard himself from trouble from Coyote.

III

Hasteen Yazzi, a Medicine Man who lives on the eastern side of the reservation gave the following mythic origin of the sandpaintings used in his ceremony of the Blessing Chant (Set III):

"The story begins with the White Shell Woman. The earth people had the chants and prayers belonging to the Hozhonji, but because they had no paintings to guide them they constantly made mistakes. The White Shell Woman told them that she would help them and have a 'sing' over herself and teach them the paintings.

"First she took them to a field of white corn. She made her foot prints in yellow pollen and then seated herself beneath a cornstalk. This stalk of corn she had planted in the center of the cornfield. Here she said all the chants and prayers and when she had finished, a bluebird came and perched upon the flower tassel of the corn and sang. In this way she knew that she had done everything perfectly.

"Throughout the night the White Shell Woman prayed and the next day she made the second painting of her house of the clouds. Again she made the house of the clouds and the seat and place for the medicine basket. This done, she took the seat and placed a medicine basket full of suds in front of her and taking off her clothes, washed and bathed her body and hair. She finished by chanting and prayers and then told the earth people that she had now taught them the paintings and to use them hereafter for blessings, crops, more children, or anything of that kind."

Notes on Approximate Locations where Navajo Ceremonies are Now Given

It has been suggested that it would be interesting to students of Navajo customs to have a list of the major types of ceremonies with the locations on the reservation where they seem to be most often given today. Sometimes the location coincides with the region mentioned in the myth of the ceremony, and where this occurs I will mention it. These notes are merely from my personal observation.

1. *TLEJI*—NIGHT CHANT, usually called the YEHBECHAI. In Klah's version of the myth (and he was considered a great expert in this Chant) the myth centered in a canyon north of the Jemez Mountains and also in the Canyon de Chelly. It is now the most popular of the complete ceremonies and is given all over Navajoland, wherever there is a priest who knows it and the people have sufficient wealth to support a nine-day ceremony.

2. *TSILTHKEHJI*—MOUNTAIN CHANT. The myth begins in the Apache country near Stinking Lake but the present ceremonies are given all over the reservation wherever there is a priest of it and enough wealth to carry through a nine-day ceremony.

3. *ATSAH*—EAGLE CHANT. The myth is centered on Tsoll-tsilth (Mt. Taylor). If any ceremonies are still given they are probably in that region.

4. *YOHE*—BEAD CHANT. The myth and most of the ceremonies coincide in location centering in the region near the Chuskai Mountains and along the San Juan River. Not often given.

5. *NILTHCHIJI*—WIND CHANT. The myth centers in the region between the Chuskai and Jemez Mountains. The many forms of ceremonies seem to be mostly given in that region and also north along the San Juan River westward.

6. *HOZHONE*—BEAUTY CHANT. The myth of this branches off from the Tsilthkehji or Mountain Chant which tells of two sisters, one of whom married the Bear and began the Mountain Chant myth. The other, who married the Snake and started the Beauty Chant, went southward toward the Hopi country where they developed the snake ceremony. The present ceremonies seem to follow the same path from near the north of Chuskai Mountains to the country near Ganado.

7. *N'DLOHE*—HAIL CHANT. The myth centers on the east slope of the Chuskai Mountains and the last priest of it was Klah who lived at Newcomb in that same region. Ceremony now extinct.

8. *TOHE*—WATER CHANT. One long myth of this Chant begins in Chaco Canyon and ends along the San Juan River, but may have a mixture in it of

Etsosi (Feather Chant). At one point it branches into the Tleji myth and the first sandpainting of the Tleji myth of the whirling logs apparently shows this connection. Another myth is centered farther west near the Hopi country and the only place where it has been given lately is between Keams Canyon and Winslow. Nearly extinct.

9. *ETSOSI*—FEATHER CHANT. The myth begins at the Pacific Ocean and then goes to a place in the north section of the Navajo country, and at present the ceremonies seem to connect with that region. Nearly extinct.

10. *N'DAH*—formerly called *ANADJI*—now popularly called "SQUAW DANCE." The myth goes back to the scalp dance given by the gods to celebrate the destruction of the monsters who were destroying mankind. The ceremony now given all over the reservation.

11. *MAH-IH*—COYOTE CHANT. The myth begins at the Pacific Ocean and goes to Canyon de Chelly and farther north. The ceremonies now are given near Canyon de Chelly and southwest from there. Nearly extinct.

12. *WILLACHEE*—RED ANT CHANT. The myth centers in the country near that of the Hopis and the ceremony is given there, but also in other parts of Navajoland.

13. *BESHE*—KNIFE CHANT. The myth stems from the Tleji. I have never heard of a ceremony though I have seen a rite of it in connection with the Shooting Chant.

14. *NAHTOHE*—SHOOTING CHANT. The myth begins in a form of the creation story. After the emergence on this earth it centers near the Chuskai Mountains. This is one of the most widespread and popular of the present day ceremonies and has many forms. Given in the form of Tsilthkehji Nahtohe, a combination with the Mountain Chant, it is a nine-day ceremony with a Fire Dance at the end.

15. *TSAHA*—AWL CHANT. I have no information on this except that it once existed.

16. *HANELTHNAYHE*. The myth of this form of creation as collected by Father Berard Haile emphasizes the powers of evil. In the many smaller versions there is a similar emphasis against witchcraft. The myth seems to center in the north towards Taos. Ceremony is very short now.

17. *HOZHONJI*—BLESSING CHANT. This is given as a separate ceremony with sandpaintings all over the reservation. It has decreased in length from a much more important and elaborate ritual to usually not more than a three-day ceremony. Certain parts of the Blessing Chant are used in connection with many other ceremonies.

18. *SONTSOJI*—BIG STAR CHANT. The myth naturally is much concerned with the sky but begins near the Chuskai Mountains and at present centers mostly on the west slope of these mountains.

Glossary of Navajo Creation Myth

Pronunciation

a as in ah   ay as in say
e as in end   ai as in aisle
i as in Inn   g always hard, as in go
o as in old   j as in English
u as in Yule   zh soft z, like French in Juliet

Nasal Sounds

anh, anse like French *an* in *tante*
onh, onse as in French *ton*
inh like French *in* in *intime*

Hyphens in middle of words to denote a separation of tone between two vowels or separating syllables, and to help in pronouncing long compound words. Proper accenting is very important in pronunciation.

In the spelling and pronunciation of Navajo words, an attempt has been made to approximate as closely as possible to an English or Latin equivalent.

A

Adáhgeh-Hasleén—
"Man Who Came Behind." He was created in the Third world.
Agay-nastáhni—
Place name for Crownpoint, N. M.
Ahchíni-bah-jee-chin—
Children's song meaning "We won't give the children away," in a game called "Protecting the Children."
Ahchíni-beyín—
Song of the children who visited Estsán-ah-tleháy on the island.
Ahdah-tintsói—
Peak on Black Mountain, near Chin Lee, Arizona.
Ahgeh-náschini—
"Black Circle." Place name near Crownpoint, N. M.
Ahn-enténi—
Pollen Bird, or Corn Bird.
Ahtsáylin—
Lies (personification).

Ahtsée-des-tseen—
Obsolete name of medicine-wand used in the Anadji or N'dah ceremony (squaw dance).
Ajah-tohée—
Poison water-weed.
Anlthtáhni—
"The Ripener;" literally Corn Beetle.
Anlthtáhni-atéhd—
"Corn Beetle Girl."
Anlthtáhni-tso—
"The Big Ripener." The Female Corn Beetle.
Anlthtáhn-nah-olyáh—
"Made from everything." Name of people created last. Man as he is now, created by Begochiddy and the Gods out of the substance of the universe in which the holy spirit had already been placed.
Arálth-tseen—
Medicine-wand used in the Anadji or N'dah ceremony (squaw dance).
Asgaí-binee—
Poison weed.
Asheén—
Salt clan.
Asheén-assún—
Salt Woman of the First World.
Asheén-assún-beyín—
Salt Woman's Song.
At-átid-éhd—
"Cornbug Girl," name of a bird.
Atráhgeh-Hasleén—
"Centre Man," created in the Third World.
Atsáh—
Eagle.
Atsáh-beyazh—
"Young Eagle," name for February.
Awáy—
Baby.
Awáy-atsálth—
Cradle of Estsán-ah-tleháy.
Awáy-está—
Baby girl.
Awáy-kiyátyeh—
"People who talk like babies." A clan left by the Gods on their journey west.
Awáy-nah-ólth—
"Baby Floating Place" in whirling waters of the Third World.
Ayáh-zush-chílly—
"Early greens are ripe." Name for June.

Ayáh-zush-tso—
"Large growth is ripe." Name for July.
Azáy—
A general term for Medicine.
Azáy-be'   hogahn—
Medicine hogahn.
Azáy-tso—
"Big Medicine." Star of December.
Ahzeth—
Place name. Rock south of Mount Taylor, N. M.

B

Bahkse-hotetsa—
"I hear about him." Place name near Mount Taylor, New Mexico.
Bakáz-tlah—
Name of playing stone.
Bászhini-éshki—
"Jet Boy." Son of the Sun by his spirit wife.
Bayéz—
Two stones joined together. Kicking stones.
Begánaskiddy—
"Bearer of seeds to men." The hunchback god.
Bégochiddy—
The great creating God, fair-haired and blue-eyed. Is masculine but his name
means "The-Love-a-Mother-gives-her-child."
Bégothkái—
Son of Begochiddy, called the White God.
Bégo-tso—
The Big God. One of the last two spirits created, whom no one has seen.
Bégo-zhíni—
The Black God. One of the last two spirits created, whom no one has seen.
Bekekeh-yázhi—
"Little Tracks." Name of Papago Indians who wear sandals with thongs be-
tween their toes who were left by the Gods on their way west.
Belthráh—
Ancestors of the Apaches who were left by the God, on their way west.
Benán-yah-rúnny—
"Staring-Eyes-that-Kill," a monster.
Bes-antsái—
Name of unknown tribe left by the Gods on their way west.
Bézh—
Flint or obsidian.
Bézh-lachée-begízh—
"Red Flint Cane." Name of Washington Pass in the Chuskai Mountains.

Bézh-l'entklízi—
Red-berried plant used for Eagle ceremony.
Bézh-'ntsah—
"Big Iron."
Bí-eth—
Laziness (personification). A black man.
Bikáy-hozhón—
Probably means "May it be beautiful."
Bikáy-hozhón-atéhd—
"Making-it-Beautiful-Girl."
Bilth-tseláh—
"Two-things-near-together." Place name of a hill south of Naschiddy, N. M.
Bínni-tahn-tsó—
"When-everything-is-ripe," and "Even-the-Mountains-are-ripe." Names for September.
Bínni-tahn-tsósi—
"Corn-tassels-have-come." Name for August.
Binskaí—
Name of playing stone.
Bitáhni—
Clan name of people created on Santa Cruz Island, California.
Bisolái—
Constellation of two stars near together.

C

Chadidoth-dáni-gosái—
Name of a blue coyote, which means "Turning-in-the-Darkness."
Chees-téhi-lakái—
Great white bird which was flying over this world when it was covered with water.
Chalth-yilth-hogáhn—
"House of darkness."
Chalth-yilth-nah-gíh-eh—
"Wanderer in the Dark." Spirit of Life in the lower world.
Chíndi—
Devil.
Chonotéen—
Name of the dance of rejoicing when Nayenezgani and Tohbachischin brought in the scalps of the monsters they had killed.
Chóostaigi—
The Fire God. Brother of Hashjaishjin.
Chustóh-ba-áhd—
"Female water."

D

Dah-gejól-gíshy—
Name of a cornfield near Huerfano Mountain, N. M., planted by the Gods.
Dáh-il-kádeh—
Huge monster which looks like a gopher.
Datá-téhe—
Humming Bird.
Datsáhni—
"Porcupines," name for May.
Dáyah-nezhón-yades-ilayah—
The song of the Beautifying of Nayenezgani and Tohbachischin.
Debéh-entsáh—
Place of the Big Mountain Sheep, La Plata Mountains, Colorado.
Debéh-neh—
Phoebe bird.
Dechín—
Hunger (personification).
Degínnih—
Holy people.
Deh-nózzi—
"Mountain Sheep People," ceremonial name.
Deh-ye-yáh-heh—
Name of a song about the beginning of Estsán-ah-tleháy's journey to Santa Cruz Island, off California.
Delzhéh—
Ancestors of Yuma Indians left by the Gods on their way west.
Dichíthli-éshki—
"Abalone Boy," son of the Sun by his spirit wife.
Dilgéheh—
Seven stars. Constellation of the Pleiades.
Dinnéh-nahoo-lonai—
Tribal name of Eskimo, obsolete.
Dinnéh-noahnai-glah—
Song of "making more people."
Dithklíth—
Black or dark.
Dobínny-des-dáha—
Ceremonial name of Dog-Who-Trails.
Do-bitsáh-hállih—
Name of Chief of Bitahni clan.
Dogo-slée-ed—
"Place-where-the-turkeys-live." The San Francisco Peaks, Arizona.
Dohgah-tyelth—
"Place-of-cutting-reeds," place name west of the Chama River.

Dóhleh—
Bluebird.
Doklízhe-éshki—
"Turquoise Boy," brought by the Sun to Estsán-ah-tleháy on the island of Santa Cruz, off coast of California.
Doklízhe-etáhdeh—
"Turquoise Girl," daughter of the Sun.
Dóntso—
Messenger between gods and men. Literally, the Whiteheaded fly.
Dont-whutsó—
"Two stars fastened together," constellation.

E

Eé-ah-eé—
Magpie.
Eékai-estáhi—
Milky Way, constellation of the month of February.
Eékai-etáhdeh—
Daughter of Estsán-nahtah.
Elkaydáhn-bayahel-gistsís—
"The beginning of the world. I am talking about it." Phrase in the Creation Song.
Elkaydáhn-shehit-taynízzen—
"The beginning of the world. I knew about it." Phrase in Creation Song.
Entklízhi-tas-éh-odolith—
"The creating of beads and jewels" in the Creation Song.
Espínee—
Game stone.
Estsá-assun—
First Woman in the First World.
Estsán-ah-tleháy—
"Changing Woman." She grows old or young at will. From her union with the Sun were born Nayenezgani and Tohbachischin who slew the monsters.
Estsán-eh-beyín—
Song of Estsán-ah-tleháy.
Estsán-nahtáh—
Head Woman in the Third World.
Etáhdeh—
Girl.
Ethkáy-nah-áshi—
"Those who go together." Substance through which breath of God passes into creation. Twins created in the Second World by Begochiddy.
Etsáy-dassalíni—
Name of the first man to die.

113

Etsáy-endit-kláhan—
"Where light rays first struck." Prayer for people who are separated.
Etsáy-enteé—
A kind of early corn.
Etsáy-etsó—
"Big Man," name of a star.
Etsáy-etsósi—
"Thin Man." Constellation of Orion.
Etsáy-hashkéh—
"Angry-Man," Coyote in the First World.
Etsáy-Hasleén—
"Man made now." First man created in the Third World.
Etsáy-Hasteén—
First Man in the First World.
Eyáh-nos-zhíni—
Prayer to help the winds hold up the world.

G

Gah-atáyjih—
"Rabbit Feet." Constellation of the month of January.
Gáhgi—
Crow.
Gáhnji—
"Half winter and half summer," name for October.
Giss—
Cane or wand used in ceremonies.
Giss-dil-yéssi—
Little rabbithrush. "Red grass." One of the four holy plants used in ceremonies. *Guttierezia enthamia.*
Gloutrah-nasjáh—
Screech owl.
Góhi-nínny—
Ancestors of the Pima Indians. Four people created near the San Francisco Peaks, Arizona, by the Gods on their way west.
Golizhí (or Wolizhi.)—
Skunk.

H

Hadach-éh—
Thing of value.
Hádahónesteen—
Name of Mirage Hogahn.

Hádahónigay-be-hogáhn—
"Mirage Hogahn," made of heat waves.
Hahdénigai-hunai—
The Emergence, obsolete term.
Hahden-nesteén-tséel—
Foggy Mountain Range, near Pacific Coast.
Hahjeénah—
"The Emergence." The Fourth or Present World. Also a lake where the people came up to this world near Silverton, Colorado.
Hahjéenah-dinnéh—
"People of the Emergence." People who came up from lower world into this present Fourth World. The prototypes of Man, Anlthtáhn-nah-olyáh. "Created from everything."
Háho-hanái—
Later dawn light.
Haltáhn-ah-begáy—
Mirage clan, left at Mirage Mountain by the Gods on their journey west.
Haltáhn-neligay-tseel—
The Mirage Mountain of Changing Woman's journey west.
Halth—
Ceremonial knife carried by Nayenezgani in the Yeh-bechai ceremony.
Has-estrágeh-hasléen—
The Second Man to Die.
Háshjéshjin—
Fire God or Black God.
Hashje—
"He who must not speak"—term used now to indicate that person wearing mask must not speak.
Háshje-áltye—
Talking God. The God who talked to man in the myths.
Háshje-ba-áhd—
Female God.
Háshje-baka—
Male God.
Háshje-hogáhn—
House God.
Hashkéh—
Angry.
Hasléen—
"Created now."
Hastéen-sikái—
"Old Man" or Swan constellation.
Hlakah-kestrah-hasléen—
"Fourth Man," created in Third World.

Hodayáh—
The Rainbow Hogahn belonging to Kay-des-tizhi in which the Creation Song was sung.
Hodayáh-dahnbíth-odolíth—
"At the Beginning Mountain-Gods made with it." A phrase from the Creation Song.
Hodayáh-dahnvén-ent-sissicasseh—
"At the beginning I was thinking about it." A phrase from the Creation Song.
Hogáhn—
The Navajo House.
Hogáhn-beyín—
House blessing ceremony.
Hogáhn-doklizh—
Blue hogáhn.
Hoosh-entseh-etsó—
"Cactus which catch people." Place name, in Canjilon Mountains.
Hóspiddy—
Dove.
Hozhónigi—
"Making the path of life beautiful." Maiden ceremony.
Hozhónji—
Blessing Chant.
Hozhón-la—
Refrain in song of Mountain spirits.
Hushklíshni—
The Mud Clan or "Near-Water-Clan," created on Santa Cruz Island, off the coast of California.
Hushkáh-bináh-oltín—
Chief of Light Waters Clan.

I

Iknee—
God of Lightning, personification in the thunderbird.
Iknee-dithklíth—
Black thunder.
Iknee-kah—
Lightning arrow.
Iknee-lakái—
White thunder.
Iknee-tsósi—
"Small thunder." Also name of month of March.
Insontzeel-odolíth—
"Creating little rain on mountains." A phrase in the Creation Song.

116

J

Jahbúnny-estsán—
Bat woman.
Jah-dokónth—
"Running-Pitch-Place." Name of lowest world.
Jish—
Medicine pouch used in ceremonies.
Jóhgee—
Mountain Bird.
Johl-eén—
Pedernal Mountain, Jemez range, New Mexico.
Johnjílway—
Poison weed. *Datura stramonium*.
Johonah-éh—
Ceremonial name for the sun.
Juggie—
Name of a playing stone.

K

Kah-dinnéh—
Arrow Clan people. Left by the Gods on their journey west.
Káhilth-klee—
Water Horse.
Kah-sah-oni-odolíth—
"Creating the arrow ." A phrase in the Creation song.
Káhtsen—
Alligator Monster.
"Kai-yolthkái-estsa-chin-eshlí-nihai-in-inyah"—
White Shell Woman's Song, meaning: "I am the White Shell Woman and I am going."
Kay-des-tizhi—
"Wound in the Rainbow," a being created by Begochiddy in the first world. Was both man and woman.
Kebeh-etéen—
"Moccasin tracks." The home of the children who went to visit Estsán-ah-tleháy.
Kétahn—
An offering to the Gods in the form of a reed cigarette.
Ketáhn-de-konth—
"Kéhtahn of Fire."
Kíh-ah-ah—
A ruin near Crown Point, New Mexico, where the Kihahni Clan lived.

Kiháhni—
A clan which orginated near Chaco canyon, New Mexico.
Kím-beto—
Place name, east of Chaco canyon.
Kin-lakái—
White House.
Ki-othkath-teeni-go-sái—
"Turning in the Daybreak," name of a kind of coyote.
Kíth-nah-ha-klíthy—
Spirit of Dusk.
Kíth-nah-klizhíni—
Spirit of Darkness.
Kláyonah-éh—
Ceremonial name for the moon.
Kleéshtso—
The Great Snake.
Klizhín—
Black.
Kloh-lachée—
Red Grass.
Konth-lachée—
Name of House of Red Fire.

L

Luka—
Reed.
Lúkachúkai—
"White field of reeds." Place name, north of Chin Lee, Arizona.
Lukasahkah-tso—
"Big Reed," place name near Alamosa, Colorado.
Lukatsó—
"Big reed;" bamboo, according to Hasteen Klah.
Lukatsó-sakáh—
"Place where big reed grows."
Luka-i-digishi—
"Cutting Reeds" monster.
Lécheh—
Father.

M

Máh-ih—
"He-who-roams-about," a thief. Name given Etsay-Hashkeh, the Coyote.

Máh-ih-besónt—
"Star of coyote."
Máh-ih-degishi—
Name of the Spirit of the Scalp. Literally, "Coyote Cane"; symbolizing authority.
Máh-ih-doklízhi-sethkính—
"Blue coyote young man."
Máh-ih-jilthli-lakái—
"White changing coyote."
Máh-ih-klitsóji-sethkính—
"Yellow coyote young man."

N

Nahasán b'hógahndi—
Creature that lives in the earth.
Nahastsán-be-esteén—
Spirit of Earth in Creation Song.
Nahastsán-odolith—
"Creating earth," a phrase in the Creation Song.
Nah-tahi-assún-odolíth—
"Creating the Spirit of Creation," in the Creation Song.
Nah-bin-ithbíthy—
Name of playing stones.
Nal-'ntsói—
"Yellow after sunset."
Nah-hodoh-óthle—
Quicksand spring in the Second World.
Nah-klitsoi-dasakah—
"Yellow-after-sunset," name of the Third World.
Naho-doklízh—
"Blue after sunset."
Naho-doklízh-dasakah—
"Blue-after-sunset" in the Third World.
Naho-kanái—
"On the Earth" people.
Nah-ketláh-tsilkoi—
Clan that wears wooden soles on their shoes, left by the Gods on their way west.
Nahotsoi-nah-gosai—
Name of a yellow coyote, meaning "Turning-in-the-After-glow."
Nahshalth-hélee—
"The Ducks," a constellation. Star of September.
Nahtah-has-éh—
Mountain south of Zuñi, New Mexico.

Nahtáhn—
Corn.
Nahtáhnapah—
Name of Medicine Man of Mountain Chant who lived near Naschiddy, N. M.
Nahtáhn-estsán-odolíth—
"Creating Chief Woman," in Creation Song.
Nahtáhn-lakái-eshki—
"White Corn Boy."
Nahtáhn-tsoi-atéhd—
"Yellow Corn Girl."
Nahtáh-tso—
"Big Corn."
Nahtáhyah-ni-zhéhni—
"Standing for the Law," ceremonial name of the boy to whom Estsán-ah-tleháy taught her medicine.
Nahtal-tilth—
Chief of the Yellow Water Clan.
Nahtéen-odolíth—
"Beginning of the World."
Nah-shálth-héhlee—
Constellation of the ducks, belongs to the month of September.
Náh-tee-tséel—
"Tobacco Mountain," near Bluff City, Utah.
Náhtoh—
Tobacco.
Náhtoh-beyín—
"Tobacco Song."
Nah-yéh-ahrúnny—
"Staring Eyes that Kill" Monster.
Nah-zunny—
Snow bug.
Nakái-John—
White John, a friend of Hasteen Klah.
Nakel-astsel-kai—
An unknown tribe west of the Navajo country.
Nashi-taythli—
Constellation of the Crown.
Nash-kónh—
Lightning struck tree.
Nashtúi-l'tso—
Mountain Lion.
Násjah—
Owl.
Násjah-Hasteen—
Owl Man.

Nasjeh—
Spider.
Násjeh-tseel—
Spider Mountain.
Nastol-dísse—
Whirling Wind, dust devil.
Natséelit—
Rainbow.
Natséen-náhi—
Substance in which Chuskai Mountain was dressed in the Creation Story.
Probably rainbow.
Nayénezgani—
"Slayer of Enemy Gods."
N'dah—
Name of Squaw Dance in the Anadji ceremony.
N'd'gilly-tso—
Big Sunflower.
N'd'lóhe—
Hail.
N'd'lóhe-lakái—
White Hail.
Nehol-zhini—
The Black Place, where one of the four clans went to live.
Nehochée-dothinlah—
Name of the door of the Hogahn-of-Darkness.
Nehochée-otsó—
"Big Hollow Place," place name, Valle Grande on top Jemez Mountains, N. M.
Neho-neh-yáhni—
Midge.
Nehopah—
Substance out of which animals were created.
Nestráhnihi—
Fire Sticks.
Nestéen-Tseel—
"Hazy Mountain," Coast Range on the Pacific.
Nezhi—
Name of playing stone."
Nicky-dol-zholi—
Name of grey ants.
Niholtso—
"Big Cyclone."
Niholtso-doklízh—
"Blue Cyclone."
Niholtso-lakái—
"White Cyclone."

Nih-othkath-teeni-go-sai—
Phrase in song; obsolete Navajo.
Níltche-beyazh—
"Little Wind or Spirit Breath."
Níltche-dil-kohn—
"Smooth wind."
Níltche-tso—
"Big Cold Wind," name for December.
Níltche-tsósi—
"Light Wind," name for November.
Níltsa-tseel—
"Moisture or Rainy Mountain." The Chuskai range.
Nohochee—
"Red Earth," where the Ant People live.
Nohokos-ba-áhdi—
"Female-Stars-Going-Around," the Little Dipper.
Nohokos-bakáhdi—
"Male-Stars-Going-Around," the Dipper.
Nohopah—
Place near Zuñi where Salt Woman went for a time to live.
Non-napáh—
"White-Shell-Woman-of-the-Future," ceremonial name of the girl to whom
Estsán-ah-tleháy taught her medicine.

O

Odolíth—
Obsolete word in the Creation Song probably meaning "Creating".
Ozeh-be-hogáhn—
Tribe of Hopi Indians north of Moencopi, Arizona.

R

Rázeh-beyín—
"Ladder Song" of the Emergence People.

S

Sahanahráy—
Holy Spirit.
Sahanahráy-bikáygi-klishín-entslée—
"Holy Spirit of Blackness." A phrase in the Creation Song.
Sahanahráy-bikáy-hozhón-odolíth—
"Creating the Holy Spirit." A phrase in the Creation Song.

Sahn—
Old Age (personification).
Sahtáh-debéh—
"Mountain-sheep-have-lambs." Name for April.
Sals-áh—
Sand dune on way to the Sun's house.
Saltáhn-iskái—
Home ofNasjah, the first owl.
Sechái—
Grandfather. A title of honour.
Sethkính—
Young Man.
Shah-beklóth—
Ray of Light.
Sháhn-deen—
Sun ray.
Shemáh—
Mother.
Sheyásh-estsá-sohni—
Woman's race in Maiden's ceremony.
Shikính—
Maiden.
Shikính-shush-nah-tléhay—
"Changing Bear Maiden."
Shonrah-hineth-hotsil—
Song meaning "my home is in danger." Sung by Bear Guard on journey of the tribes from the West.
Shush-betóh—
Bear Water. A spring near Navajo Mountain.
Shush-nah-káhi—
Bear that trails.
Shush-nah-tléhay—
Bear that changes form.
Sil-dil-húshy-tso—
Monster centipede that bites.
Síngo—
Call of Yehtso, the giant.
Sin-jay-óthy—
"Where-Water-Floats-Down-Wood." Place name near Tohatchi, N. M.
Sin-nahyáh—
Place name, "Hill-with-little-trees," near Gallup. (Modern meaning drunkard).
Siss—
Probably old Athapascan form of Tsilth—mountain (from Father Berard Haile).

Siss-báyis-kothy—
Name of woman's ceremonial medicine belt given by Estsán-ah-tleháy to the two children.
Siss-kit—
Cedar-covered flat rock near Ojo Alamo.
Siss-páli—
Place near Canjilon Mountain, Grey Mountain (?)
Síss-nah-jíni—
"Holy White Mountain of the East." Home of Begochiddy. North of Taos, New Mexico.
Síss-nah-tyél—
"Place of Much Game." Near Kimbetoh, New Mexico. Where Begochiddy created the animals.
Siss-sahkáhd—
Lone Tree. Place near Crown Point, New Mexico.
Siss-yat-yéh—
Place where Echo Spirit lives near Crystal, N. M.
Sons-she-nimmi-yah—
"Beginning-of-Journey" Song.
Sont-bidái—
Star with Horns.
Sónt-eh-dekáh—
"Star out of sight in the east."
Sóntso—
"Big Star."
Sóntso-deshyí—
"Red Star overhead."
Sóntso-dohn-doh-zéedi—
"One-that-does-not-move." The North Star, of the Month of October.
Sóntso-lah—
Star Hill, near Crystal, N. M.

T

Tabastéen—
Otter.
Tabastéen-etáhdeh—
"Daughter of the Otter."
Tabastéen-lachée—
"Red Otter."
Tahilth-lachée—
"Red Turtle" in the Third World.
Tahilth-sapái—
"Dusty Beast," the donkey.

Tahn-chill—
"Small green things." Name for April.

Tahn-tso—
"Large green things." Name for May.

Tah-zhúni—
"Smoky star," nebula.

Tas-áh-odolíth—
"Creating precious (hard) things." A phrase in the Creation Song.

Táyen—
Thinness (personification).

Tchah—
Beaver.

Tchah-toh—
"Beaver water," place near Huerfano Peak, N. M.

Toh-ah-zhóli—
"Light Water" Clan.

Toh-ashtlá-naschéen-odolith—
"Creating all mixed springs, lakes and ponds." A phrase in the Creation Song.

Toh-ba-áhd—
Rio Grande river. "Female Water."

Tohbaschíschín—
"Born from water." Brother of Nayenezgani.

Toh-bakáhni—
San Juan river. "Male water."

Toh-basdezkíh   and   Toh-basdeznáh—
Names of Hot Waters of the Third World.

Tóh-déen-da-hashkéh—
Flat topped peak in Black Mountain Range, Arizona. Connected with Etsáy-hashkeh, the coyote.

Toh-d'los-tlée—
"Water crossing place" of the Third World.

Tóhe-assún-odolíth—
"Creating Little or Female Rain Spirit." A phrase in the Creation Song.

Tóhe-egléen—
"Water Meeting place," of the Third World. Above Bloomfield, New Mexico.

Tóhe-estsán-odolíth—
"Creating Water Woman." A phrase in the Creation Song.

Tóhgay-tyelth—
"Place-of-Cutting-Reeds," near Taos, N. M.

Tohi-káth—
Water medicine plant. One of the holy plants of the Navajo. *Artemisia trifida.*

Tohini—
"Near-Water" Clan.

Toh-kai-estsán—
"Water Woman" in the First World.

Toh-klitsóni—
"Yellow Water." Clan created on Santa Cruz Island, California.
Toh-n'del-kous—
Name of period of separation of Changing Woman and the Sun after their marriage.
Tohnilái—
Dragon Fly, the messenger of the Sun.
Toh-'ntsa-estsán—
"Big Water Woman."
Téoltsódi—
"Water Monster."
Téoltsódi-lachée—
"Red Water Monster."
Tóh-o-whetsó—
Name of poison water weed.
Toh-sit-toh—
Hot Spring near Mount Taylor, N. M.
Tóh-wúlth—
Taos, New Mexico.
Trádadéen—
Pollen, typifying dressing.
Trádadéen-atehd—
Pollen Girl.
Trádadéen-bith-odolíth—
"Creating pollen." A phrase in the Creation Song.
Trádadéen-éshki—
"Pollen Boy."
Trádadéen-tsilth—
"Corn Pollen Mountain." Lake Peak, over Santa Fe, N. M.
Trádadéen   yeh-káheh-deyázh—
Pollen path between earth and sky spirits.
Tralth-kágeh-bekíndeh-nah-élth—
"House which floats on water," belonging to Estsán-ah-tleháy on Santa Cruz Island, California.
Tsa-káhn—
Big ear of corn.
Tsa-tlái—
First word of Law.
Tsáy-zhée—
Tall aromatic herb. One of the holy medicine plants.
Tsee—
Name of a playing stone.
Tseel—
Mountain. Synonymous with Tsilth.

Tséh-ah-kindithly—
"Crushing-Rocks," a monster south of Taos, New Mexico.
Tséh-altyéh—
"Echo Rock," Canyon de Chelly, Arizona.
Tséh-atéhd—
"Holy-Girl-of-the-Rock," Canyon de Chelly, Arizona.
Tséh-atehd-digínnih—
"People-of-the-Holy-Girl-of-the-Rock," left by the Gods on their way west.
Tséh-benaz-élleh—
A rock with a stream flowing around it at entrance of Canyon de Chelly, Arizona.
Tséh-bénigeh—
Rock in Canyon de Chelly, Arizona.
Tséh-bezh-delnéheh—
"Rock-with-hand-prints-on-it." Place name. Washington Pass, Chuskai Mountains.
Tséh-do-kóhe—
Place near Farmington, N. M., where the personifications of Hunger, Lice, Sleepiness, and Lies were sent to live.
Tséh-ed-áh—
"Rock-with-Wings." Shiprock, New Mexico.
Tséh-ed-áh-eh-delkíthly—
"Kicking-Rock Monster" on the San Juan river, New Mexico.
Tséh-genesh-híze—
"Place-of-Petrified-Food." In Washington Pass, Chuskai Mountains.
Tséh-gih—
Canyon de Chelly, Arizona.
Tséh-hatrál—
Place where a ceremony was held in Washington Pass, Chuskai Mountains.
Tséh-ko—
"Rock- Which-Spreads-Apart" Monster, north of Taos, N. M.
Tséh-nági—
"Rock-That-Rolls" Monster.
Tséh-nah-háhleh—
"Big-Bird" Monster, lived at Shiprock, New Mexico.
Tséh-nah-kóhni—
Place name, north of Gallup, N. M;
Tséh-n'egléen—
"Rock-Meeting-Place," on San Juan river near Farmington, N. M.
Tséh-nihi-deh-ah—
Holy place south of Zuñi.
Tséh-rahd-n'dínnéh—
"People of the Rocks." They were taught the Rock form of the Yeh-bechai ceremony.

Tsen-tyel—
Place of game aninials. Probably Siss-nah-tyel. See above.
Tsilth—
Mountain. Synonymous with Tseel, also Siss, see above.
Tsilth-assún-odolíth—
"Creating the Mountain person," who is both man and woman.
Tsilth-beel-yah—
Bill Williams Mountains, literally, "Deer Mountain." Created in Fourth World.
Tsilth-binnéh-holkóh—
Mountain where Arrow People lived, on journey of the Gods west.
Tsilth-bin-jodíthy—
Clan name of the last people to be created, "Anlthtahn-nah-olya." Now called Asheen or Salt Clan.
Tsilth-binnéh-hastéen-tseel—
Mountains on way to California. Created in Fourth World.
Tsilth-binnéh-holóneh—
"Mountain-that-thinks."
Tsilth-deltsói—
Yellow Mountain. Near Kingman, Arizona.
Tsilth-l'kai-des-káhli—
White-topped mountain where the Yuma Indians were created.
Tsilth-digínneh—
"Mountain Holy People." Lived near Crystal, N. M.
Tsilth-dilth-yilth—
"Mountain of darkness" where ancestors of the Apaches were left by the Gods on their journey west.
Tsilth-dithklíth—
Black Mountains on way to California. Created in Fourth World.
Tsilth-dohgeh-jiggah—
Mountain on the way west, where Papago Indians were left by the Gods on their way west.
Tsilth-endes-kái—
Mountains on the way to California. Created in Fourth World.
Tsilth-en-dokahnt—
Mountains on way to California. Created in Fourth World.
Tsilth-entsáh—
Big Mountain where Trailing Bear lived.
Tsilth-gantséel—
Peak on Santa Cruz Island, California.
Tsilth-il-entái—
Mountains near Chin Lee, Arizona, made in the Fourth World.
Tsilthkáh-del-káh—
Chuskai Mountains, made in the Fourth World.

Tsilthkái-des-kahli—
White-topped Mountain visited by the Gods on their way west, where the Delzheh (Yuma) people were left.
Tsilthkai-hozhóni—
"Beautiful Mountain," west of Shiprock, New Mexico.
Tsilth-kis-lakái—
"White Mountain," in Colorado. Created in the Third World.
Tsilth-kis-nakai—
Mountain on way to California.
Tsilth-klizhín—
"Black Mountain" (Chin Lee Mountain) near Chin Lee, Arizona.
Tsilth-klitsoi—
"Yellow Mountain" on way to California. Created in the Fourth World.
Tsilth-lapái-áh—
Peak north of San Francisco Mountains in which first people lived in a cave while Nayenezgani was killing the monsters.
Tsilth-lakái—
"White Mountains."
Tsilth-náh-n'deeldói—
Coloured Mountains surrounding the First World which appeared and disappeared.
Tsilth-náh-ot-zíthly—
Huerfano Peak, west of Jemez Mountains. Center of the Navajo World in the Beginning.
Tsilth-nah-tsakái—
"Half-White Mountain," visited by the Gods on their way west, where the Bes-antsai people were lèft.
Tsilth-n'doh-kunsh—
"Sailing Mountain," on way to California.
Tsilth-neeteen-tseel—
Mountain on way to California.
Tsilth-n'tso-estsán—
"Big-Mountain-Woman."
Tsilth-ran-es-tseel—
"Bright-shining or Blue Mountain," on Santa Cruz Island, California.
Tsilth-tah-del-tai—
"Third Mountain in Third World." Sangre de Cristo Range, Santa Fe, New Mexico.
Tsilth-teen-del-tai—
"Fourth Mountain in Third World." Jemez Range, New Mexico.
Tsilth-tla-del-tai—
Mountain in centre of Third World.
Tsin—
Wood.

Tsini-deh-aheh—
Mesa near San Francisco Peaks, Arizona.
Tsilth-'tsa-assún—
"Mountain Person" who is both man and woman. In the First World.
Tsis-táhilth-lachée—
"Big Red Turtle at Water Crossing Place"—in Third World.
Tsoll-tsilth—
Mount Taylor, New Mexico. Holy Mountain of the south.
Túzhi-begáy—
"Turkey tracks." Stars of April.
Tuzh-gízhi-ent-dilkízhi—
"Rock Swallows" Monsters.
Tyel—
Game animals.
Tyelth—
Bullrushes.
Tyentyel—
Flat Rock in Canyon de Chelly, Arizona.

W

Willachée—
Red Ant.
Willa-klitsói—
Yellow ant.
Willachée-tsai—
Big red ant. Wood ants half red—half black.
Willazhíni—
Black ant.
Willazhí—
Tiny black ant.
Wolizhi—
Skunk.
Wónshi—
Name of playing stone.
Wooz-cheed—
"When-Eagles-First-Call." Name for May.
Wuzzy-gíshi—
"Measuring worm." Name for July.

Y

Yah—
Body lice.

Yaah—
The upper atmosphere.
Yaah-dithklíthy-be-hastéen—
"Black Sky Man." Spirit of the sky, the Rain and Cloud Spirit.
Yaah-zheh-kih—
"Dawn Light."
Yath-pái—
Place name south of Chaco Canyon, New Mexico.
Yeh—
God.
Yeh-bechái—
"Grandfather God."
Yeh-kai-beyázhi—
"Place of the children" on the road to the Sun's house.
Yeh-nez—
"Tall God," given to the Zuñis by Begochiddy.
Yéhtso—
Giant.
Yéhtso-lapaí—
Grey Giant.
Yoh-lachée—
"Red Beads." Evil mountain in lower world.
Yolth-kái-beyázhi—
"White-shell-place-of-youth."
Yolthkái-estsán—
"White Shell Woman."
Yolthkái-etáhdeh—
"White Shell Girl," daughter of the Sun by his spirit wife.
Yolthkái-tahn—
Commeal mush ceremonially called "White-Shell-Food."
Yoódi-yenái—
Spirit Wife of the Sun.

Z

Zhan-sheya-yanez-nuchee—
Song of the body painting in the Maiden Ceremony.
Zus-entlis—
Thin-Icy-Sheet. Name for January.